Bride for Keeps

Bride for Keeps

A Big Sky Brides Romance

Nicole Helm

TULE
PUBLISHING

Bride for Keeps
Copyright © 2018 Nicole Helm
Tule Publishing First Printing, March 2018

The Tule Publishing Group, LLC

ALL RIGHTS RESERVED

First Publication by Tule Publishing Group 2018

No part of this book may be used or reproduced in any manner whatsoever without written permission except in the case of brief quotations embodied in critical articles and reviews.

This is a work of fiction. Names, characters, places, and incidents are products of the author's imagination or are used fictitiously. Any resemblance to actual events, locales, organizations, or persons, living or dead, is entirely coincidental.

ISBN: 978-1-948342-62-9

Prologue

Fall 2015

Dr. Carter McArthur had spent thirty-one years on this planet knowing exactly who and what he was and what he was meant for. The McArthurs of Marietta, Montana, were upstanding, dedicated, brilliant medical professionals. As the eldest of the three children of Dr. Gerald McArthur, he'd been born and bred to be a doctor in his own right, and he was someone no one could find fault with.

For most of his life, he'd done everything his parents had asked of him. He'd excelled in school. He'd become a doctor and had even turned down an opportunity to join Doctors without Borders despite the fact that had always been his dream. Because the most important dream, always, was being a respected, dutiful McArthur.

In his entire life, he'd only disobeyed his parents once, and that had been when he'd fallen in love with Sierra Shuller. Wild, impetuous, *tattooed* Sierra had stolen his heart at a New Year's Eve party not even a year ago. They'd been engaged within three months, married two months after that.

Marriage wasn't exactly easy, not when his mother couldn't seem to help herself from criticizing Sierra's every move, but Carter loved Sierra. And Sierra loved him. That was all that mattered. Almost six months they'd been married now, and Carter had never been happier.

But, sitting in his father's office, both his parents staring gravely down at him, Carter had a very bad feeling something was coming that would change everything.

"You've had some time to come to terms with my diagnosis," Dad said not showing an ounce of emotion.

Carter had always admired that about his father. The way he could shut out anything that didn't suit him. Carter tried to emulate it, but there were some ways he'd just never live up to his father's image.

"There's nothing to come to terms with. MS is incredibly treatable. I don't have to tell you that."

"Yes. I have a particularly aggressive form, but you're right. There are a wide variety of treatments available, though I may end up having to step down from the hospital."

"In the future," Carter corrected. "Not yet. You don't want to make any rash decisions." Something his father had said to him on more than one occasion. McArthurs didn't do rash decisions, and while his father's MS diagnosis and his keeping it a secret the past few weeks was certainly a surprise, it was hardly worth this kind of cloak and dagger theatrics.

The not telling Mom at the beginning had been ridiculous, but Dad had finally acknowledged his diagnosis, at least to him and Mom.

Now, hopefully, that meant moving forward and telling the rest of the family. Carter knew Dad hated to appear weak, and Carter supposed some might consider this condition a weakness. Still, Dad had to approach it like McArthurs approached all of their problems. Calmly. Methodically. He *was* a doctor after all. Shouldn't he be more clearheaded about the whole thing?

"No, we won't be making any rash decisions," Dad said, his mouth curving just a fraction, as if he was almost amused by his own advice being given to him. "But in the light of this diagnosis and the genetic implications, especially if you and..." Dad grimaced. "If you and your wife decide to have children..."

Carter adopted the same cool, detached expression his father had started this conversation with. "Sierra and I will start a family soon, I'm sure." They'd talked about it, though he'd suggested to Sierra she find some kind of direction for her life before they started trying. Perhaps it was cruel of him to think of his mother this way, but he didn't want Sierra to end up like her, caring only about the McArthur name and how the town viewed them and having nothing of her own.

He doubted Sierra could ever be like that. She wasn't big on caring about appearances, but he wanted to ensure she had her own avenues of passion before they started a family.

As much as he cared about his family and their approval, as much as he respected his father as a doctor, Carter wanted something...different for the family he would start. More...warmth.

Sierra was warmth personified. It was what had drawn Carter to her despite all the ways he'd known his family would deem her unsuitable. Carter had no doubts she'd be a great mother. Maybe he'd been hasty to think she needed some kind of individual direction before starting a family. She was independent and strong and—

"Biologically speaking, I'm not your father."

Carter felt like his brain flatlined for a moment before coming back too quick, too rushed. He stared at his father. "What... What did you say?"

"When your mother and I were engaged, she had an affair. You are the result of that affair."

"Wh..." He looked at his mother, but she stood there looking as placid and regal as ever. "I..."

"Now, of course this is a bit of a shock, but there have been quite a few secrets in this family lately."

"It started with your relationship with Sierra," Mom muttered.

He had kept that a secret, announcing they were engaged before his parents had a chance to manipulate things. But... "I think my parentage predates Sierra," he managed, feeling...untethered. Like he was floating above this whole thing unfolding before him. They couldn't mean he wasn't...

"Yes, well. Secrets are tearing us apart. Your brother is home thanks to Jess. We're all together as I determine what this MS diagnosis means for us as a family. It seemed important to be clear and honest."

Clear and honest. "But I..." His whole life he'd been a McArthur. The oldest McArthur.

"Your biological father is aware of the situation," Dad continued as if this was just new news, not a life-altering change to his whole perception of the world. "At this point, he has a family of his own, and we all think it would be best if we go on as we always have."

"So why... Why did you tell me?" Not a McArthur, when he'd only ever tried to be exactly that.

"Secrets. We're done with secrets. You're married now. A new generation of McArthurs is no doubt going to start. We need to make sure this next generation is raised on as strong a footing as you and your sister were. The truth is an important foundation."

Which didn't make any sense at all, since his foundation was now gone. Everything he'd believed about himself. Everything he'd been told for thirty-one years. Not a McArthur. Not made in his father's image.

The product of an *affair*. The son of a man who wanted to go on as things were, never knowing one another. "Why did you... Why would you... You got married anyway. You raised me as yours."

"Can you imagine the embarrassment?" Dad replied, as if

shocked Carter might suggest any other outcome. "Especially at the time. The stain it would have put on our name. Unacceptable. Besides, your mother made her choice. She wanted to marry me despite her indiscretion."

Carter felt sick and like he couldn't breathe. It was bad enough it didn't make any sense, that it changed his entire life, but the detached, businesslike way his father spoke about it all…

Carter didn't know how to wrap his head around it. He didn't know how to accept it.

"That's why I'm counting on you not to tell anyone until I can make a formal announcement to the whole family. We'll have a meeting to announce it in a few days and discuss how we'll move forward as a family. As much as we want to be honest with each other, this is information best kept in the family. No one need know beyond us. And I don't want you telling your wife until the meeting. I don't want you telling her at all, but I suppose I can't ask that of you."

"You suppose," Carter echoed. He felt like he had cotton in his ears and lead in his lungs.

"We'll meet Wednesday at one, if you and Sierra are available?"

"Available." Like it was a business meeting. The announcement of Dad's MS diagnosis and the fact Carter wasn't a McArthur.

"Carter, this doesn't change anything. Regardless of

blood, you are a representative of the McArthur name. I'm counting on you to keep this secret, and to behave as you always have. And to keep your wife in line. We as McArthurs are done with secrets, but that doesn't mean anyone in Marietta needs to know. Sierra must keep this information to herself or I will hold you personally responsible."

Sierra. In line. Yeah, that'd go over well. If he even uttered that phrase, his wife would go on a tear to end all tears. One that would likely end in all of Montana knowing the truth.

Dad was right though. No matter how much Carter was reeling, how hard this was to understand, he couldn't tell her before their family meeting. She'd never keep it to herself.

Why would that be so horrible?

Carter looked up at the man who'd raised him, who'd claimed to be his father for thirty-one years. Who had impressed upon him how important it was to be a McArthur.

But he wasn't. Everything he thought he was…he wasn't.

"WHAT IS THIS meeting about?" Sierra asked irritably. She hated going to the McArthur house. It was big and cold and she had always known she wasn't welcome. But she went because she loved her husband and maybe, deep down, she harbored some stupid hope they'd eventually get used to the fact she and Carter were married and nothing would change that.

"Announcements, Sierra. I've told you."

Sierra scowled at her husband. He'd been distant and grumpy for days, maybe weeks, and she thought she could handle it. Carter's brother was back after something like a decade-long absence and that would send the McArthurs into a tizzy. Whenever they were in a tizzy, Carter was... Well, he didn't like to bring her into it because her opinion of his family wasn't exactly *high*.

It wasn't a great way to start a marriage—his family hating her, her hating his family—but she loved him. That was more important than McArthur family crap.

So, if that was all it was, she would have given him his space to be distant and weird. But when he started to sound like his father, a cold chill spread through her. When it didn't let up, and he was instead snippy and quiet and... Oh, she hated this.

She sat in the passenger seat of Carter's car and folded her arms over her chest. "I don't know why I couldn't skip it. Your parents do not consider me one of your family."

"You're a McArthur, Sierra, no matter anyone's feelings on the subject. I need you there. Please..." He let out a heavy sigh. It was possibly the first display of emotion from him that wasn't all edge and silence. This was something else. Heavy. He always took on too much.

It was strange that so much of what she loved about

him—his decency, the uptight way he held himself, and all the things he took on his shoulders—were also some of the most frustrating things about him. She admired him, but sometimes she wished he'd be...mortal. Balanced. Have a flaw or two so she didn't feel like such a giant flaw compared to him.

Or maybe she just wished he'd let her in.

She unfolded her arms and reached across the console between them, sliding her hand against the back of his neck and stroking her fingers through his hair. "Babe. What is eating you up?"

He was silent, beautiful blue eyes focused on the road, jaw tensed tight. She'd never seen him quite like this, and it poked at every fear she'd ever had. Because when she'd agreed to marry Carter, she'd been certain he'd tell his family to butt out and that would be that. She'd been convinced love would fix everything. When that hadn't been the case, she'd convinced herself once they were married the McArthurs would *have* to treat her with some kindness or respect.

She'd been an idiot, clearly, and now she lived in a horrible kind of fear that eventually his mother or father would say the right combination of words to convince him he'd been wrong. He—in all his perfect, McArthur glory—didn't actually love the whirlwind of a disaster she was.

She'd confessed that to Jess the other day. Much like her, Jess was a sort of honorary McArthur—a nurse who often helped Dr. McArthur. While the family didn't treat her badly, they didn't include her either. So Sierra had become friends with Jess, because Jess didn't treat her like dirt.

Jess had told her to tell Carter her fears about his distance, and Sierra had rejected that advice. Tell him she was insecure and afraid? When he was always so sure and good and right? That would *ensure* his family convinced him she wasn't good enough.

Besides, she usually threw a little fit, and he'd come after her trying to make things right. It was the pattern of their relationship. Sierra didn't know that it was the *best* pattern, but it was always how they'd worked.

Until a few weeks ago. She'd thrown she didn't know how many fits lately, and Carter had simply *let* her. What had broken in their pattern? She didn't understand and she didn't know how to fix it.

She watched him now, silent despite her question, tight-lipped and serious, and she knew she was absolutely right when she'd rejected Jess's advice. She had to act like everything was fine. The same as they always were. It was the only way to ensure things *were* fine and would stay that way.

Carter parked the car in front of his parents' house and then he got out without a word. He didn't even wait for her before he was striding toward the house.

She stared at him for a few seconds, mouth dropped. He reached for the door, not once looking back at her. She had never seen him act this way. It was disorienting and downright scary.

She was tempted to stay where she was. His family treated her like garbage. Why would she voluntarily walk inside, especially when he didn't even seem to care whether she followed him or not?

But finally, *finally* Carter glanced back, then raised an eyebrow at her. An *are you coming?* impatient look.

It infuriated her, but worse, it scared her. They'd only been married a few months, maybe he *was* realizing the error of his ways. Maybe this was the punishment for not living up to the fake image he'd created of her in his mind, for not winning over his cold parents. Slow torture by McArthur insults.

Blinking back tears, she got out of the car and crossed the yard to him. She wished she knew what to do. How to make sure he didn't change his mind.

But all she knew to do was follow him inside, feeling scraped raw and scared.

He led her to the library where Dr. and Mrs. McArthur were sitting on the couch. Chairs had been arranged in front of the couch. Lina, Carter's little sister, was sitting on one of them. Jess on the other. Carter slid into the seat next to Lina.

Childishly, Sierra didn't want to sit next to him, but what choice did she have? She didn't want his mother sensing discord, that was for sure. If she was going to weather whatever this was, it had to be without Mrs. McArthur pouncing on a weakness.

No one exchanged any real greetings, just nods. After a

few horrible silent moments, Dr. McArthur asked Lina something about med school, which got some boring medical conversation going.

But Carter didn't speak or add to the discussion in any way like he usually did. He only stared at his hands. He hadn't been sleeping. Sierra questioned whether he'd been eating. What could be the cause of this? Something awful. So awful he wouldn't tell her. Or worse, couldn't trust her with it.

Lina looked grave as well, but not like Carter. Not like the weight of the world was on her shoulders.

So, it couldn't be that bad, could it? It was just Carter taking too much on his shoulders. Par for the course. She'd finally figure out what was bothering him and this horrible dread would go away. It would be something small and silly and he'd apologize for blowing it out of proportion once it was dealt with.

A little hush of silence fell and Sierra glanced at the doorway. Cole stood there. She only recognized him because they'd run into him on the street last week. She'd known *of* the McArthur's prodigal son who'd run away to be a rodeo star almost a decade ago, but that day on the street had been the first time she'd really met him.

Carter had been rude to Cole, and her, so she'd flounced off, not bothering to find out about the brother Carter never spoke of.

Sierra sighed heavily. Her flouncing wasn't even enjoyable anymore, but she didn't know how else to get Carter's attention when he was mired in McArthur-land. Usually a good fit got his attention, pulled him out of all he kept himself caught up in. That's the way things worked for them.

Except it wasn't working these days, was it?

Cole took the empty seat and all eyes turned to Dr. McArthur.

"Thank you all for coming," he announced, always the leader. Always in charge. Sierra wished she could admire it the way Carter did, but mostly she thought Dr. McArthur acted more like a king than a father.

She'd give her marriage into the McArthur family one thing: it had certainly allowed her a new clarity on her own parents and family not being nearly so bad as her teenage self had thought they were. Her father didn't dictate things the way Dr. McArthur did, and her mother most definitely didn't sit in judgment of everything like Mrs. McArthur did.

"Some things have been going on with the family in the past few months, and your mother and I are forced to realize we've mishandled them. Keeping my MS diagnosis a secret caused more problems than I could have ever imagined it would, and that will end now. For those of you who don't know, I've told your mother about my MS diagnosis and apologized for keeping it from her. We've decided to move forward as a family unit. Fighting this disease...together." Dad's gaze turned to Cole. "As long as we're all in agreement?"

It was a question directed at everyone, but Dr. McArthur stared mostly at Cole, the son who'd left ten years ago and was only back for a visit orchestrated by Jess.

Cole nodded.

MS diagnosis. MS. Sierra didn't even know what MS was exactly. A disease of some kind. Was it serious?

But then her thoughts turned to the fact Dr. McArthur made it sound like everyone had known about it. But no one had told her. Anything. She was the one sitting here confused and in the dark.

She looked at her husband, who didn't even have the decency to look apologetic or explain why she was the one who didn't have a damn clue what was going on.

But apparently Dr. McArthur wasn't done.

"We also decided that since some of the family knew and some didn't, that we would inform everyone of one last thing. Secrets don't make us strong, and we always want the McArthur name to be strong." Dr. McArthur looked at Carter so Sierra did again too.

He was still staring at his hands. He didn't nod or acknowledge his father, but the man continued anyway.

"After the diagnosis, after Carter was informed of it, I felt it necessary to also let Carter know that he was not my biological child."

Sierra couldn't make sense of that. She choked back a laugh, because surely this was a dream or a joke or…something.

"What?" Cole croaked, interrupting whatever Dr. McArthur had continued to say. "What?"

Dr. McArthur took a deep breath, cool and calm eyes falling on Cole. "Carter is not biologically mine."

Sierra stared at her husband, eyes wide and mouth open, and he didn't even *look* at her. He just kept staring at his hands.

Because he knew. Oh God, he'd been *informed*. He'd known these things and that's why he'd been withdrawn and… He hadn't told her why. He'd let her think *she* was the problem. That was the source of his irritation.

He'd known all these things and very, very purposefully kept her in the dark. Separate. *Less.*

"Your mother and I have spent the past few days discussing the changes we'd like to make in this family. Things have been tense. Secrets have bred that tension. As my disease progresses, it will be important for us to work together to preserve the McArthur name."

Sierra stared at her in-laws, who'd always made it clear they disapproved of her. She'd never seen them act anything but cold and cruel, but she watched Mrs. McArthur lace her fingers with Dr. McArthur's.

Sierra looked at her own husband, who was all but leaning away from her. Who'd cut her out. Even when she'd asked what was wrong. Somehow Dr. McArthur and Mrs. McArthur leaned on each other better than she and her husband did.

Sierra felt sick.

"You may each bring up any concerns you have or suggestions before we lay out the way of it," Dr. McArthur said, much like a teacher might outline an assignment in a classroom. "Jessica, you may go first as you've the least to process."

"Jess. Her name is Jess."

Sierra said it without thinking, realizing after that she hadn't been the only one who'd said it. Lina and Cole had also echoed her sentiments, along with Jess herself. Jess who never corrected Dr. McArthur.

"My given name is Jess. It's never been Jessica," she said calmly, clearly.

Strong. Certain.

Sierra had never felt more weak or uncertain or out of place in her life, and by God that was saying something. Especially in these past few months of being married to Carter.

Dr. McArthur's eyebrows drew together, confused lines digging around his mouth. "Then why did you allow me to call you Jessica for so long?"

"Because I was afraid to correct you."

Dr. McArthur blinked. "Well, then I apologize. It won't happen again. Please proceed with your concerns."

Sierra felt as though she was shaking apart. Concerns. MS. Carter wasn't even a McArthur, and he wouldn't look at her. What *was* this? Some realistic nonsense dream?

"You shouldn't dictate how we all have to handle the situation. We're all very different people and will need to deal with things in different ways. Asking for our suggestions is a step, but you need to let us go our own ways too. And don't ignore the fact that you owe us all apologies."

Suggestions. Steps. Because it was clear Jess wasn't surprised. She'd known too, at least some things. Cole had certainly been surprised about Carter not being Dr. McArthur's, but he'd known about the MS thing.

Sierra had been completely in the dark. About all of it. The only one.

While Carter, *her husband*, had known it all. And he hadn't told her *any* of it.

Because you don't belong.

Yes, people got to deal differently with different situations, but they had to… They couldn't… Sierra got to her feet, chair scraping as she scooted away. She couldn't sit here and not lose it, and she'd be damned if the McArthurs, including her *husband,* got to see her lose it.

"I can't listen to any more of this," she said, her voice breaking as she bolted for the door. She turned down the hallway. Out of the corner of her eye she saw Carter stand, grim and angry, maybe as if he was going to come after her.

No. No. She couldn't stand to talk to him right now. She would not listen to some lecture where he sounded just like his father. "Don't you dare," she said, voice shaking.

"You knew and you didn't tell me anything? Do not follow me."

She stalked down the hallway, and the tears started to fall. She pushed out of the house, realizing she had no way to get home because Carter had the keys. She let out a full sob. She didn't want to be anywhere near this place. She didn't want them to see her fall apart, but she was failing at that.

Her husband had kept humongous, life-changing secrets from her. He hadn't confided in her or trusted her. Maybe it was selfish to be hurt beyond comprehension when he'd been dealt a blow, but then she was selfish. It's what the McArthurs thought anyway.

"Sierra."

Jess's voice was calm and as much as Sierra didn't want anyone to see her this way, at least it was Jess. An outsider, like her.

"Can you give me a ride home?"

"Of course. I'm sorry this came as a surprise to you."

"He lied to me."

Jess gently touched her shoulder. "Once you have a chance to calm down a little and talk—"

Sierra shrugged the touch away jerkily. "He didn't tell me. He didn't want to. I asked what was wrong. Over and over. He let me think *I* was wrong. I thought he trusted me, confided in me. I thought he…" But all she could think was everything she'd *thought* she knew about Carter was something she'd dreamed up.

Maybe he was someone else entirely.

Or he'd just finally figured out she wasn't worth the effort.

Chapter One

February 2016

SIERRA LOOKED AT the calendar blindly. Five months to the day. Five months since that stupid, stupid meeting. And every month since on the fifth she looked at the calendar and hoped *this* month would change things.

But it had been five. More months than she cared to admit of acting like a petulant child. Yelling and drinking and embodying the kind of horrible sideshow the McArthurs were hideously embarrassed of. She would have made a major ass of herself at the rodeo in September if Jess and Lina hadn't stepped in.

It had been satisfying. Sort of. Except Carter had withdrawn further and further, and she didn't want that. No matter how scared she was that everyone was right—theirs was not a marriage meant to last—she still loved him. Withdrawn and distant, hurt by his actions, she still loved him.

So, on New Year's Eve, a year after they'd first met, first kissed, she'd made herself a promise. No more tantrums. No more embarrassments. She'd do what Carter wanted, because maybe it was what he needed after finding out his life was built on a lie.

She'd become the perfect McArthur clone this year. She didn't argue. She didn't speak out of turn. She didn't ask why he spent some nights with his parents, and she didn't complain about his extensive hours at the hospital or with his father. She didn't ask him for more, or tell him how much she missed him. She didn't beg him to touch her, because *God* he hadn't even tried to hold her hand in months. *Months.*

After all, what was worse? Hurting and having him or hurting and not having him?

For these few months of good behavior, the answer had been that not having him was worse—the pain of shrinking herself into something small and stifling seemed worth keeping him.

But this wasn't keeping him, was it? Every day that ticked by she hurt more, and he got further away and...

She looked at the five on the neat little calendar he always kept hanging from a clip on the refrigerator. She'd been awful. She'd been good. Nothing had changed. Didn't that tell her everything she needed to know?

Her behavior didn't matter. *She* didn't matter to him. Nothing she did would change what he did, and didn't that mean she shouldn't keep hoping for more? She wasn't good enough for him. She'd known that anyway. So, didn't that mean she had to end it?

Her thoughts revolved around that horrible word these days. *End.* Carter had never uttered the word *divorce*. He barely uttered any words, and likely McArthurs didn't *do* divorce no matter how unsuitable the wives chosen were. After all, Dr. McArthur had married Carter's mother even knowing she was pregnant by another man. Because pride and reputation were more important than anything else.

Carter was different than his father. Sierra *knew* that even now, but as the door squeaked open and she looked at the handsome, if drawn, man who still made her stomach swoop, she wondered if it mattered. If he ignored those parts of himself—the differences, the emphatic heart—it didn't matter that they existed.

If he saw her the same way his parents did, none of this mattered, did it?

"Hi," he offered stiffly as she simply stood in the doorway of the kitchen, staring at him. She felt like crying, but that was one of those emotional responses she'd promised herself to stop having in front of him.

She'd save that for later after he fell asleep. If he was even staying here. She'd cry herself to sleep either way.

How was this her life? How could she keep on like this? And yet…just like Carter didn't speak the word *divorce*, she didn't leave. She stayed and contorted, because she kept hoping she could do something to make him love her again.

But maybe that was impossible.

She couldn't bear the thought, and she didn't know how

to tell him. That her heart was breaking. That she was miserable. Wasn't it obvious? He was miserable too. But if she opened those floodgates, she was afraid she wouldn't be able to stop and she'd lose him all the same. Afraid he'd confirm all her fears about herself.

She didn't know the magic combination of words to make him stay without risking that, so she stayed silent.

"Hi," she finally replied, her throat tight and her eyes burning with tears.

"I, uh, just stopped in to change. Dad asked me to stay over again. Mom's…struggling."

Sierra kept her mouth shut, though Mrs. McArthur's martyrdom of Dr. McArthur's illness was already old. MS was hardly a death sentence, that much Sierra had gleaned from reading up on the disease. It certainly didn't foretell Mrs. McArthur's own death. It made no sense she needed constant support from Carter.

And see—wasn't that the thing? This would have come between them regardless of the real father thing. The secrets and the silences. Even if things had been good, Carter would always want to support his mother no matter what she was going through, and Sierra would think she was a dramatic jerk.

They were *doomed*, regardless of this particular incarnation of that doom.

Carter walked through the living room and toward the hall that led to their bedroom. Sierra followed, though she couldn't explain why. Panic beat in her chest.

She was going to lose him.

She'd already lost him.

But he was here in their bedroom, shedding his suit jacket as he moved toward the closet.

"Did you need something?" he asked, sounding exhausted and desperate for her answer to be no.

You. I need you. But she didn't know how to admit it in words. She'd lost all the words in practicing her silences. So, she stood there, desperation clawing at her in an all new way. Five months. *Five months* of no talking, no smiling, no kissing. *Five months* of nothing but shadows.

She wanted that irresistible light she'd seen in him when they'd first met, that amazing, inner warmth that had made her forget everything he was, and everything she was.

It had started with that. Warmth, light, and a kiss.

Maybe there was some way it'd bring him back. She shook as she crossed to him, and she couldn't have explained why kissing her husband seemed like some revolutionary baring of her soul. Why she felt sick with hope when it would be easier to speak, to ask, to demand.

But words…words could be used as weapons, and she'd used her own as weapons enough. A kiss was the only thing she had that didn't come with a million other pieces of baggage.

So, she walked right up to him, closer than they'd been in months. She touched his shoulder, watched as his eyebrows drew together as he glanced down at her hand there.

Then she did what she considered the bravest thing she'd ever done. She rose onto her toes and pressed her mouth to his. Firm, but gentle, her eyes screwed tightly closed to keep her courage up.

When she fell back to her heels and managed the courage to look up at him, he was standing exactly where he had been, his expression exactly what it had been when she'd touched his shoulder. Baffled.

"What was that for?"

But he didn't say it accusingly, and there was no censure in his gaze. It was all confusion. She didn't know what to say, so she did it again. Pressed her lips to his, let all of her love and worry pour into that gentle meeting of mouths.

He was still but not stiff, accepting but not responsive exactly, but this time before she could pull away, he touched her. The lightest brush of his fingertips down her shoulder, then the light pressure of his palm on the small of her back.

She shuddered, hope and relief infusing the moment, prompting her to stay here against him longer than she had with the first kiss.

Finally, his mouth moved against hers, a subtle adjustment so his bottom lip brushed her top one, the slightest flick of his tongue against the seam of her mouth.

She wanted to cry with relief, but instead she moved, pressing herself against him fully. Throwing herself into the kiss more wildly, more insistently, and in that moment it was as if something ignited between them. A desperate heat and need she wasn't sure had ever been there even before all this mess.

She should dissect it, except she didn't want to. She wanted to burn in it as his tongue swept into her mouth, as his arm banded her tighter to him. She wanted to forget *everything* and exist where kisses and attraction were simple. Elemental.

They didn't talk. She had the fleeting thought they should, but then his hands moved under her shirt, smoothing up her abdomen to her breasts and she figured they could talk later. After all, what was more enjoyable? Exposing horrible emotional wounds or the way he devoured her mouth, a starving man desperate for her?

Her. He hadn't stopped *wanting* her at least. And she wanted him. She tore at his clothes, and that seemed to set him off so that he was pulling hers off too.

It was different than it had ever been. Edgy and desperate. Maybe even a little angry. They'd always had good sex, but it had been happy, enthusiastic sex. This was something…darker.

She didn't mind. Not at all. It made her feel powerful instead of weak, important and elemental instead of inconsequential and small.

They fell to the bed, panting and naked, a tangle of limbs. She crawled on top of him, and she guided him inside, watching as their bodies joined in one long, slick slide.

She gasped. It had been so long and she'd forgotten somehow in the weight of all this awfulness that it could feel good, feel right, to be joined with another person. With *him*. Even when things didn't work, *this* worked. Sierra and Carter worked.

She moved against him, but she didn't look at him. Fear tangled with all that pulsing want, and she was afraid if she looked at him it would feel like goodbye. It wasn't an end. It was a hope. Skin to skin, heart to heart.

She had to believe in hope. They wouldn't be *here* if he didn't feel something for her.

He rolled her over, strong and in charge as ever, the complete opposite of what he'd been the past few months. This was Carter. *Her* Carter.

She reached up and touched his face, allowed herself to look into those blue eyes she loved so much. They were cloudy with desire, his mouth and jaw hard, and there was a moment where she wanted to say something important. Tell him she loved him and that she needed him. Something, anything. Cement them here where things made sense.

But he moved, ruthless and knowing, making words jumble in her head. The orgasm crashed over her in a rush, and he followed on a pained groan, deep inside of her.

He dropped his forehead to hers, something he'd always done in the aftermath. That intimate touch a sign. A promise.

They could fix this. They could. She sighed contentedly. They *would*. None of this would have happened if things were hopeless.

But when she woke up later in the dark, she was alone in their bed. Carter was gone. His coat. His shoes. Him.

He'd left without a goodbye—not long after she'd fallen asleep if she had to guess by the fact it was only three in the morning.

She lay there for she didn't know how long, the heavy weight of the truth finally getting through all her fears, all her love, and all her hope.

They couldn't fix this.

***

CARTER STAYED AWAY for a week. It was cowardly. He knew it, and he also knew he should be disgusted with himself for the way he'd bungled things.

He shouldn't have slept with her. Not now. He wasn't in the right frame of mind. He hadn't been able to fully…cope yet.

She deserved a man whose world wasn't upturned by a family secret. A man who didn't struggle to sleep and eat because he couldn't fathom not being what he thought he was.

It was wrong to have given in until he could find a way to fix this dark fog that had enveloped him. He needed to be at his best for her. Strong and in control and the man she'd fallen in love with, not this strange...shell.

But fixing this feeling, emerging from this darkness was eluding him, and he didn't know how much longer he could simply...exist. But what other options were there?

Like he had for five months, he came up completely and utterly empty. Him. The man who was supposed to be smart and able to diagnose most anything couldn't find his own solution to his own problem.

"There you are."

He glanced up at his sister as she strode into the hospital cafeteria. *Half-sister.* Lina only had a few months left of her residency here, and Carter didn't think she had plans to stick around Marietta once that was over.

He wondered if Dad had figured that out with everything else going on. Or had Lina used the diagnosis and aftermath to hide her plans? Because their father would *not* be happy if she left.

Her dad. Not yours.

"What the hell do you think you're doing?" Lina demanded, fisting a hand on her hip. He'd never envied that edge of hers before, but here in this moment he did. He envied her certainty and her strength when it felt like all his had been sucked out when his father had delivered that blow.

You aren't really a McArthur. Everything he'd spent thirty-some years trying to be. She was. Cole was. He wasn't.

"Carter," Lina repeated.

Carter pushed away his thoughts, looked down at his untouched dinner. "I'm...eating dinner." Sort of.

"With your *wife*, you idiot. What the hell are you doing with Sierra?"

Carter didn't look up from the cafeteria sandwich. "That isn't any of your business." Even the mention of Sierra made his brain shut down, leaving a numbness. His body and brain refusing to deal with the pain that ached there. A protective mechanism.

Lina huffed. "For someone who isn't actually Dad's blood relation, you sure do sound like him."

He flicked a glance up at her, but that tiny glimmer of anger faded so fast he wasn't even sure it was real beyond all the numbness.

"What is *wrong* with you?" she said. "That *should* piss you off. Sierra wanting to divorce you *should* scare the hell out of you."

"She doesn't want to divorce me," Carter replied, without really thinking the words through. But, she couldn't want...that. Things were bad, but she'd initiated that night last week. She wasn't going to leave him.

She couldn't.

"Carter. She's been to a lawyer."

"That isn't true." It couldn't be. They'd... They'd slept together. Yes, it had been a mistake and yes, he'd walked away and stayed away for a week, but it meant she cared. She'd made vows. She was supposed to stick with him through thick and thin. That was how this worked.

"You need to talk to her, or you need to get professional help. Actually both."

"Professional help?" He stared at his sister blindly.

"You're depressed."

"I'm not *depressed*. I'm..." Fine wasn't the right word, but he couldn't come up with an alternative that fit what he was feeling.

"Are you sleeping?"

"I—"

"No. Anyone can see that. Eating?"

"I eat."

"Not enough. Are you enjoying your work, work that you've always enjoyed, or are you just going through the motions?"

"I..." He was sure her point was wrong, and yet he couldn't find an adequate defense of how he was feeling, or his actions.

"You're depressed, Carter. Talk to your wife, or talk to a therapist, or, like I said, both, but you have to talk to someone. You have to...do something. You can't keep being this." She made a hand motion that seemed to encompass his entire being.

Talk to someone? That didn't change anything. His life was still upended, and talking only ever... He needed to handle this like his father did. Strong. Sure. Calm. Once it was handled, he'd be able to act. "I'm handling it."

Lina shook her head and handed him an envelope. "Then why am I handing you divorce papers?"

Carter could only stare at the envelope.

"Sierra came here wanting to give them to you herself, but she... Anyway, she asked me to do it. And I agreed so I could try and talk some sense into you."

"I'm having the worst year of my life and she wants to divorce me?" Divorce. It was hard to make his mouth even move to say that word, because that word conjured up images of a life without Sierra and...

Haven't you been living a life without Sierra?

"Do you think about anyone but yourself?" Lina asked disgustedly, tossing the envelope next to his tray and onto the table. "Have you given even five seconds of thought to anyone who's also affected by all this, or is it only about poor Carter?"

This time the spark of anger lit and stayed. "I have been busting my ass to take care of Mom. I have been—"

"Hiding," Lina finished firmly, looking down at him with such *contempt*. His little sister who was forever trying to one-up him, and he hadn't even had to try to make it impossible.

Except she's his and you're not.

"You've been an ass and a coward, and maybe some of that would be forgivable if you cared about anyone but yourself, but I guess I've been wrong all this time. You are just like Dad, biology or no. Nurture versus nature, right?"

And with that, his sister turned on a heel and stormed out of the cafeteria, leaving quite a few eyeballs trained on him.

A spectacle.

Not a McArthur.

Divorce.

Whatever anger had ignited at Lina's accusation of selfishness evaporated in an instant. He looked at the envelope and tried to picture his life without Sierra in it. Even these past few months when everything had been an awful void, she'd been there. Some little sparkle of hope that a day might come when it didn't feel like his whole life was falling in on him. She *was* his hope. The thing that kept all the going through the motions worth it.

At some point he'd wrap his brain around this. He'd feel normal again. Life would... It wouldn't stay this way. It couldn't. At some point it'd click again. They just had to be patient and wait for that to happen.

So, no. He refused to accept it. They were not getting divorced.

Now he just had to figure out how to make sure of it.

Chapter Two

March 2016

SIERRA LAY ON an air mattress in a cramped room in her sister's apartment where she'd been staying for far too long. It wasn't right to put Kaitlin out like this, not for these three weeks since Sierra had packed a bag and walked out of her home with Carter. She wondered if he'd even noticed.

Regardless, she hadn't been able to bear the thought of seeing him while she'd been getting divorce papers drawn up. She hadn't been able to hand him the divorce papers, even if it made her a coward. And even though it had been two weeks since Lina said she'd given them to him, she hadn't heard a peep from him and the papers had not been filed.

She'd have to face him. She knew she'd have to face him, but every day she woke up in this tiny room that was already decorated for the little girl her sister would have any day now. She woke up and her head felt like it was full of cotton. She was exhausted and achy and sure she was coming down with some weird flu that never fully hit.

She blew out a breath and looked at the changing table where she'd set her rings last night. She'd tried to sleep without them. It had been fitful, and even this morning she desperately wanted to put them back on.

Desperately wanted to go home and find Carter and say she didn't mean it. She'd sit quietly in the corner and never say anything just so long as they were together.

Not that he'd filed the damn papers, which meant if she really wanted to she could walk back into their house and pretend like the past three weeks apart didn't exist.

The fact she *could* do that made everything harder. There was only so long she could wait. Once Kaitlin had the baby, Sierra was on her own. Which inevitably meant moving in with her parents, which…

God, she was tired of being their little failure.

A knock sounded on the door and Sierra forced herself out of bed to open it. She had to brace herself against the doorframe as a wave of dizziness came over her.

"You okay?" Kaitlin asked, eyebrows drawn together in concern.

Sierra managed a nod. "Just a little light-headed, I guess."

Kaitlin's concern didn't disappear from her face, but she smiled. "I made some breakfast. You probably need to eat."

"I should be making you breakfast," Sierra said, feeling utterly awful for taking advantage of her pregnant sister like this.

Kaitlin waved it away as she walked, well, in fairness, waddled to the tiny kitchen. "I'm uncomfortable and need to move. I'm *restless* and it's too cold to be wandering the streets—at least that's what my husband tells me."

"Where is Beckett?" Sierra asked, shooing Kaitlin out of the way so she could at least *serve* breakfast even if she hadn't made it.

"Went in to the shop early. He's got the next few days off for the impending arrival." Kaitlin patted her large, rounded belly. "So today he's trying to finish up a few projects." She awkwardly lowered herself to a chair.

Sierra got out two plates and tried to ignore the panic at the thought of Beckett being on vacation from work and Kaitlin having her baby and the fact the only place Sierra had to go was her parents' house.

Because she had no job and no skills and hadn't even tried to do anything except survive the crushing weight of failure and pain of losing Carter.

"I can't thank you enough for letting me stay here so long," Sierra managed to croak. Because what would she have done if Kaitlin hadn't offered her this little respite? If Kaitlin hadn't offered some semblance of friendship, which was something they hadn't had since probably elementary school if even then.

"It's been nice. I'm sorry for what you're going through, but it's been nice to…be friends. And really you've been indispensable around here. Helping me with baby stuff, and the whole getting up out of chairs things. If you hadn't been here I would have been stuck on the couch day in and day out waiting for Beckett to come home."

It wasn't true, but it was sweet of Kaitlin to say so. They'd never been particularly close, but if Sierra had gotten anything out of this shitty few weeks it was a new camaraderie with her sister. Kaitlin wasn't as hard as she used to be, happily married and about to pop, and Sierra knew she'd changed herself too. Matured in some ways. Or at least was in the process of maturing.

"Still no word from Carter?" Kaitlin asked carefully.

"No. He's waiting me out." He probably knew. That she didn't want to lose him. That she was a coward. Probably thought he could ignore the papers and live in this horrible space of nothingness forever. Well, she wouldn't let that happen. No. She needed to find her courage. She needed to find her spark again. "He probably doesn't think I'll fight dirty." But maybe it was time.

"Surely he knows you better than that." Kaitlin smiled, though it was immediately interrupted by a wince.

"You okay?" Sierra asked, not envious of anything her sister was going through physically, even if she'd been pestering Carter about starting a family before the whole...implosion had happened. The reality of pregnancy in front of her made the prospect of a chubby baby to cuddle a little less appealing.

Besides, that wish had been mostly wanting something to bind them together, and wasn't that warped? Sure, she wanted to be a mother, and so much of that had come from wanting to see Carter as a father because she thought he'd be such a good one.

Apparently she'd been wrong. About everything.

"Just starting to get a contraction here or there. The doctor said not to get excited until they're more regular, but God I hope this is the beginning. I want to walk normally again."

Sierra turned to face the stove where Kaitlin had placed a pan of perfectly baked cinnamon rolls. Sierra should be happy and excited for her sister. Eager to meet her niece. But all she could think about was the fact she was about to be evicted.

Sierra shook her head and plated two rolls for each of them. She turned to put them on the table, but something in the smell hit her all wrong. She wrinkled her nose as a wave of nausea hit her. She wished this damn flu thing would just go away already.

She put Kaitlin's plate in front of her, and sat down with her own, but she couldn't stomach the thought of eating it.

"I know you like cinnamon rolls. What's with the pained face?"

Sierra shook her head. "Oh just this same thing. Some weird bug I guess. Maybe I'll go to the doctor tomorrow."

Kaitlin nodded, but she kept staring at Sierra with a speculative look on her face. "I have a weird question to ask you."

"Shoot."

"It's just, maybe because I've got pregnancy on the brain but light-headedness, nausea, exhaustion...everything you've been having the past few weeks. I know it could be the stress and emotional upheaval of everything with Carter, but those can all be signs of pregnancy too."

Sierra laughed. "Yeah, right."

"Are you sure you couldn't be pregnant?"

Sierra started to laugh again, because you had to have sex to get pregnant, but then her laugh died. There had been that night. No protection and she'd stopped renewing the prescription for her birth control pills in the five months of hell because it had felt like a cruel joke to bother.

Pregnant.

"So, it's possible?"

Those words hung in the air and Sierra couldn't truly wrap her brain around the actual reality of it. *Possible* seemed to echo in her head, over and over again.

"Shit," Kaitlin said on a gasp, pressing her hand to the side of her rounded stomach.

"What? Another contraction?"

"No." Kaitlin blew out a breath, and then sucked one in. "Well, yes, but I think... I think my water just broke."

CARTER HAD TAKEN a few days off from the hospital. He'd ignored his mother's phone calls. He'd holed himself up in his house to finalize his plans. He was good with plans, with schedules, with figuring out all the steps to get what he wanted.

However, the goal of *staying married*, wasn't so easy as *passing the MCAT* or *getting the right residency match*. Those had steps to follow, books to read on the subject. It wasn't foolproof science, but it was close.

There was nothing about Sierra or relationships that was foolproof science. Or had any steps to follow that made any sense to him.

Occasionally over the course of trying to figure out how to fix this mess, he'd wondered if it was worth it. If divorce was the answer. It was what Sierra wanted, and didn't he want her to be happy most of all?

But he thought of his life without Sierra in it, and even though it didn't make any sense, even though he was stable and methodical and laser focused and she was mercurial and spontaneous and pure fun, he loved her. With everything he had. He'd married her—this whirlwind of vivacious *life*—even knowing his parents disapproved, even knowing just about *everyone* thought it was a joke. He'd done this one rebellious, spontaneous thing in his whole life because he'd *had* to. There had been no other way, no other choice. She was a magnet and every particle of his being was drawn to her.

He just didn't know what to do with it all, how to show *love* or care. He'd never seen it in action, not really. He knew bedside manner, though it wasn't his best quality. He knew how to pick the right words when it came to tell someone they needed to see a specialist, or be admitted, or even that the future looked stark.

He didn't know how to explain love, to put into words this big, horrible thing inside him. It was too messy. Too unpredictable.

He looked down at his desk. It was a mess of papers—mostly computer printouts of his calendar, though there were a few lists. Apology gifts. Second honeymoon ideas. A grand anniversary gesture.

He hated grand gestures and attention, but Sierra didn't.

And this was where he came to at the end of every thought. Gestures and gifts didn't solve the problem. He couldn't think of anything that would because he didn't know why the problem had happened. He was trying to fix symptoms of something bigger, but he didn't know what that something bigger was.

He crumpled up a piece of paper and threw it across the room, which only frustrated him more because paper was hardly a satisfying thing to throw. So, he went about reorganizing his stacks of papers for the who-knew-what-th time.

If he kept looking, he'd find the answers there, in neatly piled stacks and organized thoughts. Lists and calendars held the answer, *somewhere*, because they were the things he understood.

Except once he'd finished making everything look neat

and organized, and he stared down at his desk that had all the right electronics and pens and *things*, he didn't feel any of the ordered relief.

Because Sierra still wasn't here.

He frowned, broken from that horrible train of thought by the creak of a door, and the soft sound of what *had* to be footsteps.

When Sierra appeared in the doorway to his office, he briefly considered the possibility he'd had a break with reality. Except she looked a little too pale for a fantasy, and her expression was grim rather than happy. Surely if he was losing his mind, it'd at least be with a happy Sierra.

"Hey," she said, and her voice sounded raw. In fact, everything about her looked a little raw. She wasn't wearing any makeup, which was rare for her—she didn't like to leave the house without it. She was wearing a baggy sweatshirt and sweatpants and her golden hair was pulled back into a haphazard ponytail. But the most disorienting thing was the utter flatness in her brown eyes. A complete lack of spark, which had always been that thing that had drawn him to her.

"You're back."

"No." She let out a bitter laugh. "I'm not *back*, Carter. You haven't filed your answer, and I have a life to move on with."

Carter ignored that and gestured to the armchair in the corner. "Sit. We should talk." He settled himself at the seat behind his desk. This was perfect, really. A calm, rational sit-down to work this all out.

She stared at his desk, his perfectly arranged papers, but she didn't sit. She just stood there and stared at his desk as if it was some horrifying foreign object.

"Sit," he repeated, because maybe she hadn't heard him. Maybe she needed to be encouraged. "Please."

"No." She shook her head, that bitter laugh escaping her mouth again, making him frown. "No, I won't be doing that."

"We need to talk," he emphasized, changing the *should* to *need*, because it *was* a need, not a request.

Her eyes flicked to his, still so flat and blank, and no matter that her laugh was bitter and her frown harsh, her eyes were just…empty. "No, we don't *need* to talk. Not anymore. You had months to talk and you didn't and I'm not going to sit here and having a *meeting* with you, Dr. McArthur. I won't be lectured or talked *at*."

"Sierra—"

"No." She hugged her arms around herself and shook her head vigorously. "I won't do this. Not when you use your father's exasperated, condescending voice on me. That heavy sigh as you say my name." Her gaze held his, and there was a tiny spark. Something he didn't recognize though. Not her usual light. "*That* isn't love."

"I'm not talking about love," he replied, very calmly and reasonably if he did say so himself.

"Yes, I'm very well aware."

He closed his eyes in pain for a moment. "That isn't what I—"

"I'm pregnant," she said, not giving him a chance to explain anything. She cut off all rational thought with that…bomb.

Pregnant.

He opened his mouth to say something, but he didn't have words. Throughout his residency and his, albeit still rather short, career as a doctor, he'd had to break all manner of horrible news, and he knew the right words for that.

What words were there for this?

"That night…" She swallowed and it was the first sign of something like nerves. Sierra. Nervous. He wasn't sure he'd ever seen her that way. "Well, I hadn't been taking my pills for a while. There wasn't much point, was there?"

"That night was a mistake," he said reflexively. She looked stricken, and he realized she didn't understand that either. If she'd only give him more time, he wouldn't be ruining all this. "I didn't—"

"Well, regardless, I still want the divorce. You're the baby's father, so you'll be involved once he or she is born, but there's no point in being married while we do it."

"No…point." Anger sparked, cautious at first but growing rapidly as if every second that ticked by was a steady dose of oxygen for the blaze. For once, the numbness didn't win. "Of course there's a point, damn it. We're going to have a baby, a child." A child. His child. He was going to be a father. A father. "Marriage *is* the point."

"I'm not your mother, Carter. I have no interest in being miserable for the sake of the children, or whatever her whole life has been about. I didn't marry you to be a McArthur or to be ignored or silenced or… No. So, I'm going to build a life I love." She met his gaze, chin tilted, determination in her shoulders-back stance. "Which means not being a McArthur."

I'm not a McArthur, he wanted to say, but none of this made sense. A child. Divorce. A future. An ending.

"I'm not signing those papers." It was the one piece of truth in all this chaos. The one stark, black *fact* in all this gray area. "Filing. Whatever. I'm not divorcing you."

"I didn't want to make this ugly, Carter. But I will."

"We are not getting divorced," he said, standing so he could have those inches above her. So he could look down at her and make certain she understood. This was his proclamation. They would not do this awful thing she was suggesting.

But she laughed in his face. "Watch us," she said, and then turned on a heel and walked out of his office.

Chapter Three

"SHE'S PRECIOUS," SIERRA said, though her throat felt too tight. The tiniest little bundle in her arms looked like a squished alien, and yet she *was* precious.

Beckett sat next to Kaitlin on her hospital bed and Sierra and Kaitlin's parents sat on a little couch in the corner. Their brother, Luke, and his wife, Melanie, stood next to them. They'd all taken turns holding little Ellie.

Sierra didn't want to let her go, though she knew it was time to leave. Time to face the music.

She wasn't going back to Kaitlin's apartment tonight. Well, she supposed it was morning now, a whole new day. The day before had been a whirlwind. The morning with Kaitlin going into labor, Sierra driving to the next town over to get a pregnancy test during the wait for Ellie's arrival. The box had told her it was too early to tell, and still she'd been determined to see that negative sign and feel some relief even if not total.

But there'd been a positive one instead. Early and everything.

Her life had changed in that Walmart bathroom, and

she'd driven straight home to the house she and Carter had shared once upon a time, to tell him. She'd felt no more wishy-washy wondering if she should suck it up, wait him out, whatever.

She'd just known, in that crystal-clear moment of a positive pregnancy test: her life had to change. She was going to have a baby, and even if something happened to it, she didn't ever want to go back to being the version of herself who'd crawled into a little box the past few months and basically given up.

No. Life was going to change.

As she held the newborn in her arms, she knew she couldn't even begin to fathom how much. But she was determined to be ready. To be strong. Maybe her whole life had been one of failure, but she would not fail her child. If she promised herself nothing else, it would be that.

Which meant giving Ellie back to her exhausted but joyous parents, telling her own parents she was moving home for a while, and... Well, she wasn't ready to tell anyone but Carter about the pregnancy yet. Not so early. But she'd start preparing nonetheless.

"We should let you two get some sleep," Mom said, a clear nudge in Sierra's direction to relinquish her hold on the baby. "Well it's you *three* now, isn't it?"

Sierra forced herself to turn to Kaitlin who sat in the hospital bed, puffy face and bags under her eyes, and yet with the kind of contented smile Sierra wanted to find for herself.

She'd never have it with a man who shut her out, who clearly saw her for what she was. She would need to be someone other than what she was for her child, and she couldn't do that with Carter at her side. He was too perfect, and he'd always remind her of that.

When Ellie began to fuss, Sierra murmured, "Here's your mama," and Ellie snuggled into Kaitlin's chest. Kaitlin met Sierra's gaze and lifted her eyebrows, a clear question.

Sierra gave a quick nod and Kaitlin reached out and gave her arm a squeeze. Simple as that, her sister was offering support. And to keep quiet about it. A sister Sierra had never been all that kind to. They'd been too different, but it didn't seem to matter now.

Even in the sadness of knowing she had to move on from Carter and all the failures of the past year, there was a kind of hope in that. Things could change. Things could get better. Maybe not marriage things, but life things.

She shuffled out of the room with her parents and brother and sister-in-law, murmuring goodbyes to the happy couple and the fussing baby. A nurse gave them a kindly smile as she slid through the door while they exited.

Sierra trudged with her family through the hospital and toward the parking lot. She was sure it was just paranoia that it felt like every person they passed in the lobby stared at her.

"We're over this way," Luke said, pointing to the far side of the parking lot. The family said their goodbyes and though Sierra was parked somewhere in between the two, she trailed after her parents.

"Um, Mom and Dad. I... Would it be okay if..." She shoved her hands into her coat pockets, too hot in the face with embarrassment to feel the chill of the air around them.

Mom and Dad turned, exchanged one of those old married couple looks that caused a lance of pain to go through Sierra's chest. Even at their best, she and Carter hadn't had that.

Mom enveloped her in a hard, warm hug. "Have we really made it this hard for you to say you need to come home?" Mom sounded...hurt, almost. Which was odd. Her parents were always so stoic. She knew what they were feeling based on what they said, not what they sounded like.

"No, I just..."

"We're sorry things didn't work out, Sierra," Dad said, in his same old gruff way, but the words were soft somehow. Her father who'd never been particularly soft. "I know we weren't exactly supportive, but I hope you know we always support *you*."

"Who told you?" she managed to ask.

Mom cleared her throat, twisting her fingers together in a rare sign of unease. "I overheard some nurses talking about... Well, they said Dr. McArthur's wife was leaving him. At first I thought they meant Gerald, but that seems unlikely and now you're asking to come home, so..."

"We're getting divorced," Sierra forced herself to say,

bald and plain, because she couldn't take her parents trying to convince her she was wrong. Telling her she had to fix things. "I know your feelings on divorce."

Mom and Dad shared another look.

Dad cleared his throat. "I know we've been hard sometimes. It was the way we were raised, the way we thought it best to raise ours. We're trying to be a little better by you three these days. I don't support divorce unilaterally, no, but...like I said, Sierra, we'll always support *you*."

"Follow us home. It's too cold to talk in this parking lot like this. We'll make you some... Goodness, what time even is it? We'll eat a meal and you can talk to us and tell us what you need."

Sierra blinked at her mother. When had her parents changed? Opened and softened? Asked her what she needed?

She frowned a little because she had this horrifying thought all of a sudden that it wasn't *them* who had changed. It was her. Like she'd grown up a little and realized the world, and they, weren't out to get her.

She forced a smile and a nod and headed for her car, where she'd already thrown all the things she'd taken to Kaitlin's, to follow Mom and Dad home.

But Mom's words kept bouncing around in her head as she drove through the bizarre morning that felt like it should be night after being in a dark hospital room for a while.

Tell us what you need.

She wanted to. Tell her parents everything so they could

fix this for her, but she knew they couldn't, but worse, so much worse...

What if she didn't know what she needed?

※

CARTER NEVER GOT drunk. There had been very few times in his life where he'd flirted with the edge of it. The night he'd met Sierra and his wedding night were about it. A little tipsy on alcohol and Sierra, both times. But that was very much it. He was a McArthur, expected to be in control always.

After Sierra had dropped her pregnancy bomb, then sauntered away so certain divorce was an inevitability, Carter had sat at his desk and stared at his lists.

It had been strange to sit there and not want to make new ones. He'd felt empty and numb and filled with zero desire to make a list or fill out a calendar. He couldn't even find it in himself to do the math to figure out when their baby—*baby*—would be due.

Sometime around midnight, something inside of him had clicked. Maybe snapped. He'd gotten up, walked straight to the kitchen, found a sealed, expensive bottle of liquor his father had given him for some occasion or other. Carter didn't even bother to read the label to see what kind it was.

He just started to drink. Right out of the bottle. There

wasn't much point to stopping either. There was no one to perform for. It didn't matter if he got drunk because there was literally no one here who cared what he did.

Something cracked inside of him, only it wasn't all that painful. Maybe it was the booze running though his system, but it almost felt freeing. He didn't have to be perfect for his father—who wasn't even his father. His mother had two other children to rely on now that Cole was home for good, and quite frankly, they were the children she hadn't lied to their whole lives.

And Sierra was gone. Pregnant with his child and *intent* on divorce.

It didn't make any sense. Alcohol didn't either, he supposed, but the addition of quite a bit of it into his system made that seem rather funny instead of soul-crushingly awful. He managed to drink his way through a good three-fourths of the bottle over the course of the evening.

He watched the sun rise through the kitchen window in a drunken stupor and then figured he might as well burn all his plans. They were ash anyway. Luckily, the living room fireplace only required the flip of a switch and he had a nice little blaze.

Sierra had complained about the gas fireplace, saying a wood-burning one was so much more *authentic*.

"But it doesn't do for the drunken burning of things, does it, babe?" Carter said into the empty room, grabbing a handful of the lists and printed papers off his desk. He marched back to the living room where the fire danced easily if not *authentically*.

He dropped the papers on the floor, then picked up one sheet of paper. The second-honeymoon ideas. He tossed it in. Then his calendar where he'd planned out a timetable of when he'd win her back by.

Goodbye, calendar. Goodbye, lists. Goodbye, life.

It was very lucky he was drunk, because he didn't have the wherewithal to panic at the fact his life was over and gone. He didn't have to worry it felt that way even though he had a job—an *important* job. The kind of job only people like him could do.

Except he'd believed that because of all that McArthur blood coursing through his veins. He'd believed he was offering a service to the world because that was the McArthur way.

He wasn't a McArthur.

He wasn't a McArthur.

Months of that sentence marching around inside of him, and he'd never allowed himself to fully form the words. Say it. He'd been too numb, too horrified. So he'd simply let it sit there on the edges, much like Sierra.

"I'm not a McArthur," he forced himself to say aloud and into the fire.

Carter slowly lowered himself to the floor, something horrible and clawing working through him. An emotion he couldn't push away, something like a sob if he was the kind of man who cried. The kind of man who broke.

But he wasn't that. Except when he rubbed his hands over his face, sitting on the cold floor with the heat of his fake fire on his face, his palms came away wet, and that horrible, clawing feeling dug in deeper and worse.

So, alcohol was in fact a terrible idea. No more of that. No, he should have thrown himself into work. That was familiar. That wasn't dangerous or confronting. It didn't bring all his shields down and force him to face an ugly truth that he'd messed this all up on his own.

It took three rings of the doorbell for him to realize that's what the sound was. He managed to crawl to his feet and stumble to the front door.

There seemed to be two or three doorknobs to choose from, which of course wasn't possible, and still he couldn't focus enough to get a hand on the knob on the first try.

Third time was the charm and he managed to swing the door open. In his drunken state, he didn't know who to expect. The couple before him in the soft morning light was at the bottom of that nonexistent list though.

His brother stood on his stoop, Jess standing next to him. It was so strange to stand here and realize he was more like Jess than Cole. Jess had been a foster kid who'd befriended Cole in high school, and because of her nursing aspirations, Dad had taken her under his wing.

Carter might as well be a foster kid to his father, meanwhile Cole—the screw-up rodeo star who'd refused everything Dad had tried to mold him into—was actually a McArthur.

Jess's eyes widened and she looked up at Cole. "He's drunk." Jess looked at the watch on her wrist. "At eight in the morning."

Carter laughed at the comically shocked look on Jess's face. Cole didn't look quite so shocked, but then Cole didn't know him. Not really. They were acquaintances at best. Carter used to think it was his superiority that kept them separated—as much as Cole running away to rodeo for almost ten years—but maybe it was that lack of McArthur blood to bind them.

"Half brother," Carter mumbled.

"What's that?"

"We're not *brothers*, are we? We're *half* brothers."

"So?"

Carter shrugged and turned away from them both. He stumbled a bit as the floor seemed to tilt underneath him. Luckily the wall came up out of nowhere to hold him up and steady. "To what do I owe the visit?"

"Mom's worried."

"So, she sent you." Carter collapsed onto the couch. Standing seemed like too much, too hard.

"No. She sent Lina. Who refused. But then asked Jess to check in on you, and I figured I should come along."

Carter stared up at the white ceiling. "Why'd Lina refuse?"

"It isn't important," Jess said gently.

Cole sat himself at the edge of the couch, easily knocking Carter's legs to the floor, though Carter managed to keep his body on the cushion. "She said you're a self-centered ass who hurt her friend and she won't pander to your sorry bullshit."

Jess sighed. "It wasn't important," she grumbled. "It isn't time to take sides."

Carter squinted up at Jess who hovered there above him at the arm of the couch. She and Cole had been high school sweethearts before Cole had taken off for the rodeo. But now they were a couple again, somehow figuring out their past mistakes and finding love. Here and now.

Why did *they* get that?

"You'd take Sierra's side though if it was time to take sides." He didn't bother to phrase it as a question. Sierra might not have won over his parents, but Sierra, Lina and Jess had formed some sister-ish bond. "You both would." Because there was no love lost between him and his brother. He sat up, his head going fuzzy and wishy-washy, but that didn't change the spark of emotion inside of him. "Only I didn't do anything. I don't know why she left. I didn't *do* anything."

"Maybe that's the problem," Jess offered.

"Relationships are hard work," Cole said seriously, as though he had any idea.

"I suppose that's why you shirked yours for ten years," Carter said, and even drunk he knew it was too harsh, but he didn't need his younger, half-brother's lectures when he *hadn't* done anything wrong. And Cole hadn't been here.

Cole's mouth firmed, but then he nodded. "I suppose it is." Cole studied Carter and Carter merely scowled.

"Have you ever had to try hard at something?" Cole asked.

Carter bristled, because that wasn't a real question. It was one of those questions where the person was so sure they already had the answer. Except who had been here the past ten years? Who had stayed by Mom and Dad's side? Certainly not Cole. "I have worked my *ass* off for years to—"

"Working hard and trying hard aren't always the same thing, Carter. You might have put in a lot of hours, a lot of sweat. Obviously you worked hard to become a doctor, but was any of that a struggle for you? Has anything ever been a struggle? A failure you had to overcome? Or is this the first time life said: not so fast, hotshot?"

Carter pushed off the couch. "Fuck off, Cole."

"Look, I know you don't want to hear it from me, but I am just trying to help."

Jess reached out, touching Carter's arm lightly. "Have you talked to anyone—really talked—about how you're feeling?"

"I'm feeling drunk, Jess. It's quite nice."

"Carter—"

"My wife is leaving me." He opened his mouth to go on. My *pregnant* wife is leaving me. Except... He didn't want to expose himself that deeply. "How am I supposed to feel?"

"Sierra loves you. I know she does." Jess looked torn. "But love requires a certain amount of communication."

Cole stood, and Carter was struck by how much his brother looked like him, even though he hadn't seen him in years. Even though they were polar opposites in doing and thinking, they were so similar physically. All Mom—blue eyes and blond hair. Their differences had to have been the differences in their fathers.

Carter felt…defenseless. Except he had a defense. A million of them. "I didn't do anything wrong. I don't know why she left. I don't know what you want from me."

"You mean… You haven't talked about *why* she wants a divorce?" Jess asked, sounding slightly horrified.

"I told her we needed to talk and she said I'd had all the time in the world to talk and it was too late. What am I supposed to do with that?"

"I think you're supposed to talk."

Carter glared at his brother. "Why are you of all people lecturing me?"

"Because I've had to learn a thing or two about opening up and talking."

Cole and Jess exchanged a look that made Carter's stomach turn. He hated when people did that. He and Sierra had never mastered that art every other couple he knew had. To simply look at each other and know what the other was thinking.

He refused to believe it was because he didn't love her, or because they'd rushed into marriage, or any of the other things his parents would happily ascribe it to. It was just he and Sierra weren't built that way. It didn't mean they didn't belong together.

Except, here they were, very much not together.

"If there is anything Dad taught me, it's that you have to fight for what you want. Getting onto the rodeo circuit was never easy. Coming home wasn't and still isn't easy. Hell, a relationship with Jess isn't easy, and that's still a hell of a lot easier than any relationship with Mom or Dad. You've had a lot of easy, Carter, no matter how hard you've worked. But now it's time for the hard stuff, and I know deep down, there's a man who can take it on."

"How on earth do you know that?" Carter asked, that horrible clawing feeling growing inside him again. That awful sob-like thing building up inside of him.

"I know not being Dad's is a blow," Cole said in a quiet, serious voice that disturbed Carter if only because his brother was usually stoic and determined. Hard. There was a softness to this. "But regardless of the blood pumping in your veins, who you are and how you act are your decisions to make. You're like him because you've wanted to be, but maybe it's time to open your eyes to what you know deep down. You're not as cold and hard as he is. You never have been, no matter how hard you've tried. I'd say if anything your marriage to Sierra proves that."

"I only ever wanted to be him," Carter whispered, staring at his hands. Hands he used to think were just like Dad's. "He was always...right."

"No, he just thought he was and made everyone too afraid to cross him."

Carter lifted his gaze. "Except you."

"We're different people, Carter. Not because of our blood, but because of our souls. Whatever in your soul prompted you to fall for Sierra and marry her, whatever part of your soul is causing you to drink and lose control over the loss of her, that's the part you need to follow."

"But that part feels powerless and stupid and weak."

"So make it strong. It's either that or lose Sierra."

Carter looked into his brother's blue eyes and felt something like brotherly kinship for the first time in their lives. *Make it strong.*

What a strange concept. Foreign. But losing Sierra wasn't an option, so maybe it was time to find some other side of himself.

Not a McArthur. Not what he thought he was or even what the knowledge he wasn't Dad's blood son had done to him, but Carter McArthur. Owner of this body, this soul.

And desperately in love with a woman who didn't want his last name—a name that wasn't even his.

It was a mess. A terrible mess, and while he wasn't any good at cleaning up messes, like Cole said…

Maybe it was time to start.

Chapter Four

SIERRA WOKE UP in the bed of her youth. The dogged flu feeling, which was apparently pregnancy, seemed ever present and if not growing worse with every day, certainly not dissipating any.

And every day she was faced with the knowledge she was living at home, working on getting divorced, growing a baby and being utterly unemployable. Her work experience was a series of failed retail and waitress endeavors that had ended in her getting fired because she never could quite control her mouth.

She'd had an Etsy store for a while, of paintings and drawings and little things she'd made, but the anxiety of figuring out what to sell and how to price it hadn't been worth it. Especially once she'd married Carter and hadn't needed to make any money. She'd been able to volunteer here and there whenever she'd felt like it, and she had planned on that and motherhood being her life.

She'd been an idiot.

She had no doubt Carter would do whatever it took to take care of their child. She would never have to fear her child wasn't taken care of or fed, but there was the tricky thing of having to provide for herself. Having to figure out what she could possibly do that would make her child proud of her, and support herself as best she could.

Sierra groaned and rolled over in bed. One thing was for sure—she couldn't keep torturing herself like this. She had something like eight months before the baby was actually here, and she had to take the steps to build a life.

Maybe it wouldn't be so bad to stay here. Mom could help with the baby, and Sierra would find a way to be helpful in a way she hadn't been as a rebellious teen. It'd give her the time and space to find some kind of job that would work around having a baby.

Determined, she flung the blankets off of her and went to the closet where she'd thrown her bag. At some point she'd have to go get the rest of her things from her home with Carter, but she wasn't ready yet. Maybe once she could go a whole day without having her rings on.

She looked down at the glittery bands on her finger and told herself to take them off. To start now. Be strong.

But she couldn't bring herself to do it. Once she was feeling steadier physically it'd be easier to do. Once Carter filed the divorce papers. Once things felt more…permanent. She was sure it'd get easier and pushing herself to do it wasn't necessary at all.

One day at a time. Self-care. Being kind to herself.

She pushed the closet door open, then simply stood

there. On the top shelf, was a pile of her old sketch pads. Next to it, old canvases and paints. Once upon a time she'd fancied herself an artist.

Dad had been less than thrilled, always telling her to find a more productive hobby. Something that might land her a job. Something stable.

She'd balked at that, but now she understood, sort of. Supporting herself was far more important than she'd ever realized. Dad might have been harsh and a little closed-minded, but he'd been looking out for her welfare.

Art would never really support her, but maybe if she got back into this hobby she loved she'd find some piece of herself. She needed to find some source of strength, some source of…wanting to move forward instead of giving in to this horrible gray world that lay before her.

She pulled down a sketch pad and a pencil. She'd just sketch something. See if it all came back to her. Free her mind and let some emotion pour out. It'd be a good outlet. Cathartic even.

She settled herself cross-legged on her bed, took a deep breath in and out, and then just…let herself sketch. Just like she used to do when she was an angry teenager. She didn't think about what she was drawing or why, she only *did*.

Until it started to take shape. She scowled down at the square jaw and half-smiling lips.

Why was she drawing the bastard's face?

A knock sounded on the door and Mom popped her

head in, looking fretful. "Sweetheart, Carter's here. I thought I should let you know before your father chases him off with a hunting rifle."

"That hunting rifle hasn't been loaded in twenty years."

"No, but he's banking on Carter not knowing that."

Sierra looked down at the sketch pad, then up at her mother. Determined, she set aside the pad. "I'll handle Carter," she said, getting to her feet.

"Are you sure?"

"If I'm going to…divorce him, I have to have the wherewithal to face him." It was still hard to get that word out, *divorce,* but she'd made her decision. She would not let her parents fight her battles for her.

"Erm, you're still in your pajamas."

Sierra looked down at the baggy flannel sweatpants—his—and the shapeless sweatshirt, which she realized with a wince was also his. "All right. Have him sit down in the kitchen and I'll be down in a few. And please keep Dad and his fake rifle away."

Mom smiled, though it was a little sad around the edges, before she left the room.

Sierra immediately moved into action. She didn't want Carter to think she was lying around in her—his—pajamas all day. She got dressed, put on a light coat of makeup, and fashioned her hair into a messy bun that hopefully fooled him into thinking she'd spent time on it. She even slipped her feet into her cute ankle boots and headed downstairs, chin held high.

She'd pretend she was on her way out. *So* busy. If her heart beat too hard and too fast, and her eyes felt a little teary, well, she'd never let him see it. She sailed into the kitchen trying to find her center of righteous fury.

Carter sat at her parents' kitchen table. They hadn't spent much time with her family. She hadn't wanted to. Her parents' house was so small compared to the McArthurs'. Shabby. She hadn't thought much of it, but she'd been embarrassed.

Which was gross. They might not have as much money as the McArthurs, but her parents were good, kind people. They would have treated Carter far better than his parents had ever treated her.

"Sierra," Carter offered, his tone giving no hint as to why he was here. He was dressed casually, though crisply, and he'd clearly shaved this morning as no golden whiskers glinted in the morning light streaming through the window above the sink. His hair was a little long, but he'd brushed it.

He looked very polished and together. The perfect Dr. McArthur. She wanted to put her head into his lap and ask him to forget about everything. She'd go home with him and they'd pretend the past few months were a bad dream.

But that wouldn't make her life better. It'd only make her miserable even if it gave her a few moments of relief.

"Have you filed your answer?" she asked by way of greeting.

"No," he said, watching her with a gaze she didn't quite recognize. There was something too...assessing. As though he'd woken up from his months-long fog. But even if that were possible, she couldn't let it change her mind.

They were getting divorced. It was the best, happiest route for both of them, even if it hurt like hell.

The bottom line was her father had always been right. Love and dreams didn't solve real-world problems.

"Then I don't know what on earth you could be here for."

"I'd like to talk," he said, and luckily he kept that continually maddening calm because it made her angry.

"Yes, well, we've been over that."

"Right. I suppose it's your right to not want to talk."

"You suppo—"

"But you have to understand, Sierra. I don't get this." There was enough bald emotion in his tone to make her freeze. "I don't know why you left. Why you're so angry. I'm lost. Maybe it makes me a fool, but I have to know. What went wrong?"

Sierra sank into the seat across from him. Exhausted and nauseous and incapable of mustering any more righteous indignation. "If I have to tell you, does it even matter? If I have to spell it out then it wasn't working, was it?"

His eyebrows furrowed and she had to link her fingers together on the table to keep from reaching out and smoothing the tips against the line that wedged there. She always called it his McArthur line and kissed it away.

She couldn't do this. Not *this*. Not just sit here and talk. It hurt exponentially to sit across from him and feel that ache of how much she wanted to be with him.

It was a horrible feeling to want something you knew was toxic, something you knew hurt you, just because it felt good in the moment. There were good moments in her marriage with Carter, but in the end she'd emerged less than a year later a duller, quieter, less sure version of herself, knowing he saw through everything to the parts of her he'd never love.

"Please go. Please file the papers. You can't stop the divorce, Carter, but it'd be so much easier if you just did this. Please. If you care about me at all. Please make this easy."

He stared at her across the table. Not at her exactly, but at her hands. She curled her right hand over her left and looked away from him.

"Five minutes a day," he said, his voice soft but certain.

"What?" she replied, wrinkling her nose at him.

But he had that McArthur look about him. Driven and sure, except... She couldn't explain it, but it *was* different. Maybe it wasn't sure so much as determined. She couldn't work that out, and there was no point in working it out. She had to move on from figuring Carter out.

"Five minutes a day for a month. You give me five minutes a day for a month to win you back."

She wanted to scream, or lean forward and bang her head against the table a few times. Instead she sighed heavily.

"There's no *winning*, Carter. It just didn't work."

But he kept on like she didn't exist, just as he always did. "Five minutes a day for a month. If you're still determined to end it—end this thing... You know, you *know* it's right. I know you do." He reached across the table and took her right hand away from her left, exposing her rings still there on her finger. He brushed his thumb across the bands.

She used every last ounce of energy to keep the tears from spilling over. "You don't know everything, Carter."

He met her gaze then, and it wasn't anything she recognized. "No, I don't," he said gravely. "You're saying if I care about you that I should make this easy, and I'm saying if you care about me, you'll give me a month. Five minutes out of your day for a month. That's it."

"Why should we prolong the inevitable?"

"Are you so certain? There's not an ounce of doubt that you might regret this at some point?"

She wanted to tell him she *was* that certain. Maybe he even loved her the way she loved him, but the love they had for each other wasn't enough to make a life together work. Their lives didn't work together, regardless of love.

"Shouldn't we be sure?" he asked, his hand closing over hers and giving it a squeeze. "If for nothing else, for the sake of the baby," he whispered, as if he knew her parents were probably eavesdropping but wouldn't hear that.

She pulled her hand away, placing both of them in her lap. He was mixing it all up and she should be stronger than this, but part of her wanted... Well, she wanted him to find a way to convince her otherwise.

She couldn't think it was going to happen, but maybe she could hope. "Fine. Your five minutes starts now."

Oh, she was going to regret this.

<hr>

HE'D EXPECTED HER to agree, but he hadn't expected her to jump right into it. He wasn't quite prepared, but he couldn't let her see that. He had to seem certain and sure of everything so she believed him.

"How are you feeling?" he asked, because she didn't look 100 percent. She was more put together than she had been the other day, but she seemed...off.

"Gross," she said emphatically. Because Sierra was brash and not backing off and not worried about what she was supposed to say.

Maybe that's what drew him to her. That she had an independence to her that he'd never be able to emulate, but was attracted to nonetheless.

But the clock was ticking and he had to figure out the answer. The fix. Five minutes even for thirty days wasn't much, but it gave him till their anniversary to find the answer to why she wanted to leave.

And then he could fix it. Maybe he'd fail a few days along the way. Maybe it'd be hard and more of a challenge than he was used to, but Cole had been right. It was either stumble a little but keep trying, or lose her.

He wasn't ready to lose her. Even if she pulled her hand away from him like they were strangers or enemies instead of man and wife.

He cleared his throat, willing himself to focus. "Who's your doctor?"

"No. I'm not having you McArthur your way into that."

He wanted to argue, even opened his mouth to lecture her about privacy laws and this and that, but what was the point? Making her mad was *not* the point. "All right." He thought about her hand under his and the glimmer of hope that he'd hold on to this entire thirty days…assuming it took that long. "Why are you still wearing your rings?"

She inhaled loudly, then looked down beneath the table, presumably at her hands in her lap. "I take them off sometimes, but I guess they start to feel like a limb. Something is missing when I take them off." She looked back up, fixing him with a rebellious glare. "That doesn't mean anything. I'll get used to having them off eventually. It's habit, not symbolic."

"Okay," he said carefully. Maybe it didn't mean anything to her, but it meant something to him. He looked at his ring on his finger. A simple gold band. "I remember when you put this ring on my finger," he said, more to himself than to her. It was visceral. The happiness he'd felt when they'd slid their rings onto each other's fingers in front of their friends and family. He hadn't cared at all that his parents didn't approve or that hers questioned the timing. He hadn't cared about anything except her being his. "I remember our vows."

Sierra rolled her eyes. "Vows, like promises, are apparently meant to be broken."

"I haven't broken mine," he replied, trying to keep his temper from lighting.

"Haven't you?" she retorted.

"I loved you. I was there for you."

"There for me? No, Carter. You were there for you, and you were there for your mother." She stood, her chair scraping loudly at the jerking, violent movement. "You were always happy to be there for *everyone*, but you never once—"

It was his turn to stand violently. "I love you. I supported you. I gave you a very nice life and we were together. What more did you want?"

She shook her head, and it pained him that tears shimmered in her eyes, but he didn't understand why all the blame was being heaped on his shoulders when he didn't see things the way she did. At all apparently.

"I'm not going to have a screaming match with you. I'm not going down this pointless road of blame and memories. We don't work, Carter. I had to accept that. Now you do."

"You always do this," he said, realizing it so much in the moment he couldn't even make his tone sound less accusatory. "Any conflict and you say you're not going to do it. You shut down and walk away."

"*I* shut down? How can we even get to the conflict? You haven't engaged with me in months. *Months.*" She fisted her hand on her heart and if he wasn't so damn angry he might have kept his mouth shut. Instead, he did what he almost never did. Made a nasty, sarcastic remark.

"The baby you're carrying seems to say otherwise."

She paled, her hand going to her stomach. Some kind of hurt flashed in her eyes before she blinked it away and lifted her arm. "Get out," she ordered, pointing to the door.

"Sierra." He took a step toward her, but she turned her back to him.

"You had your five minutes. Now go."

"This was different. We never fight. We never yell. Not at each other. Not like this."

"Why would anyone want this?" she asked, and she didn't even wait for his reply or anything else before she walked away, down a hallway.

Carter let out a slow breath. That was…something. Something new. No, it wasn't any fun, and no it wasn't the stuff good marriages were made from: blame and anger and nasty comments.

But it was different. Something like that trying hard Cole had been talking about. Which maybe meant it was the right step.

Someone cleared their throat and Carter looked up to see a furious-looking Mr. Shuller and a blank-expressioned Mrs. Shuller.

"Don't come back here. You understand me?" Mr.

Shuller said gruffly.

Carter managed his professionally blank doctor smile. "Yes, sir." He walked through the small living room and to the front door, letting himself out as he stepped into the cold winter air.

He tugged his gloves out of his pocket and pulled them on just as the front door squeaked open. He looked back expecting to see Sierra, hoping to chase that strange feeling the fight had given him.

Instead, Mrs. Shuller stood there without a coat on, hugging herself against the cold. "Maybe I could have Sierra meet you somewhere for your five minutes tomorrow?"

Carter raised his eyebrows. Clearly Mrs. Shuller had been listening. "You listened?" Had she heard about the baby?

Mrs. Shuller looked a little abashed at that. "I happened to overhear a few things. Not everything."

It didn't answer his question, exactly, but it didn't matter. Everyone would know eventually. "And..." He tried to wrap his head around what she was offering. "You're going to help me?"

"No, I'm going to help my daughter," Mrs. Shuller said firmly. "I don't know about fixing your marriage, Carter. I'm not sure I ever had much belief in that. But I think you two should discuss why it's ending."

It wasn't what he wanted to hear. He wanted her belief and her support, anyone's really, but he'd settle for her help. "If you could have her meet me at Java at noon?"

Mrs. Shuller nodded. "She'll be there."

Chapter Five

"Mom. Seriously. I am not in the mood for...anything."

"It'll do you some good to get out and walk around. I promise."

Sierra doubted it. She'd rather wallow. All her determinations from yesterday were gone after the fight she'd had with Carter. She just wanted to *mope*.

They never fought. It was all she could think about. She and Carter never fought. It was one of the things she loved about him. She could go off the handle and yell and stomp and he'd calmly, placidly take it. He'd smile or give her a hug. Not give anger and frustration right back.

It twisted everything up. It made her *hurt* to watch him get angry or defensive or think he was right and she was wrong. It brought up childhood memories of watching Dad and Luke fight bitterly. The feeling was the same—twisted up and uncomfortable, wishing the conflict would just go away. She'd learned to run away from that. When Dad had been mad at her as a teenager, she snuck out. Partied. Anything to keep her mind off *conflict*.

Why on earth was Carter giving her conflict now? When they should just walk away from each other and be done with it? Love didn't matter when your life wasn't working, and how could love exist when you were yelling at each other?

Sierra *hated* this. Mostly because she couldn't control Carter's reaction. She couldn't make him not care. She couldn't make him walk away.

Why *was* that when he'd been, at best, a robot for months? When he'd made her feel like he'd finally figured out what a horrible match she was for him? Now all of a sudden he wanted to understand it and fight for it?

She didn't know how to make sense of this, and what's more, she didn't want to. Better to end it, even if that was running away. Fresh starts would be better. For both of them.

She sighed and looked out the window as Mom parked a little ways off from Java Café. The prospect of walking into the little café, seeing people she knew, seeing people Carter knew—

"Mom. Really. I can't."

Mom put the car in park and looked over at her. "Okay. You stay put, I'll go grab us some sandwiches, okay? Maybe even grab some to take over to Kaitlin and Beckett. I need my Ellie fix. What do you think?"

"Yeah, okay." Even though thinking about babies was a little daunting, it was better than thinking about her feelings and all the conflict inside her.

Mom smiled and got out of the car and walked across the street to Java. Sierra hunched in her seat and looked at her lap. But that only occupied her for so long and eventually her gaze drifted out the windshield. Above the squat brick buildings that lined Main, Copper Mountain stood looking stately and important against the impossibly blue winter sky.

As a teenager the sight had filled her with dread. Like that mountain was always glaring imperiously down at her. Like God, very much displeased with her decisions.

Now it looked like any other mountain. Neither evil nor benevolent. Just rock and time.

When the driver's side door opened Sierra tried to fix a smile on her face as she glanced over at her mother. Except it wasn't her mother sliding into the driver's seat so soon after disappearing inside.

"What the hell do you think you're doing?" she demanded.

Carter didn't blink, flinch or act like this was completely inappropriate. "Our five minutes," he replied as if this was some plan she'd agreed to.

"No."

"It was a deal, and your mother agreed to stay inside for precisely five minutes, so we really should start talking."

"It was not a deal, or if it was, I changed my mind."

"But I didn't."

She crossed her arms over her chest and glared at him.

"And you're all that matters?"

"Of course not," he replied easily and sensibly. A Carter she recognized, down to the way his blue eyes seemed to match the sky. "But if it takes two to start a marriage, it should be the agreement of two to end it."

"Actually, I think that's generally not how that works."

"Regardless. All I'm asking is five minutes today. Is that really so much of your day?"

She looked away. It wasn't. She just didn't *want* to keep feeling this awful. She wanted to move on. To be done. She didn't want to fight or rehash or give him the opportunity to convince her into another mistake.

Everyone said they were a mistake. They always had. Why shouldn't everyone be right?

"I don't want to fight," Sierra said, looking straight ahead. Facing down Copper Mountain. It suddenly felt like that old disapproving presence again.

"I thought it was interesting," Carter said, and she'd call it his doctor voice. Detached and inherently practical. Like he was dissecting a frog and telling her about it. "I've never really fought before. I always strive to be the better person. I figured I was supposed to be."

There were a few silent seconds and Sierra told herself not to look at him, but her eyes apparently didn't get the brain's message. He sat there, staring at the steering wheel with his eyebrows drawn together. He looked…sad, and it *hurt*.

"There were a lot of supposed tos," he murmured.

"I was very much a *not* supposed to." They'd been stupid to ever think Carter McArthur would survive a not supposed to. That wasn't his fault. She knew he'd married her because he'd wanted to, and maybe he even still loved her, but she'd been stupid to think she could change him when it came to his family. She'd been stupid to think she'd be just as important to him when she'd always been so much…less.

"I never regretted my one not supposed to."

She wanted to tell him it wasn't about regrets, but she knew her voice would be little more than a croak. And she'd cry if she said anything more than that. She didn't want to cry in front of him and show that weakness he already suspected about her.

But Carter reached through the space between them, his fingers brushing across her jaw before he cupped her cheek with his hand. She wanted to lean in to that. His hand was big and warm and she'd always found comfort in him. He'd always been the one person in the world who could calm the storm inside of her.

But he'd calmed it so much she didn't even know who she was anymore. She couldn't dwell in that when she was going to have a son or daughter to raise next year. She had to find the storm. Navigate it. Harness it. She had to find some strength and certainty.

It could never exist in the McArthurs' world, and he might not be a McArthur by blood, but that was still his world by deed. It was still where he belonged. What he loved. If he loved her too, it was in a smaller way.

She was the not supposed to that didn't fit.

Though it felt like a cracking inside her chest, she flinched away from his touch and leaned against her door. "Don't." She shook her head, trying to shake away that slow uncurling warmth inside of her.

"If you still feel something when I touch you—"

"It isn't about..." Sierra closed her eyes. "I don't want to feel this way. Any of these things. I don't want to argue with you about them. I just want to be left alone."

"We'll have to deal with each other when the baby comes."

"And we will." She opened her eyes, focused on that strength and will inside of her. She had to trust it. Grow it. "With a divorce between us," she said certainly, because that divorce felt like a shield from all this feeling. If she could keep it up, if she could separate herself from him, she wouldn't feel all these ugly things.

He sighed and leaned back in the chair. Mom tapped on the window and Sierra could see the apologetic smile on her face.

She tried to work up anger that her mother had conspired with him, but as Carter opened the door and got out all Sierra felt was that hollow feeling expanding, the darkness inside of her enveloping just about everything.

"What time tomorrow?" Carter asked, his deep, confident voice cutting through some of the dark.

She couldn't possibly take more. "I'm not doing this tomorrow."

"I'll come by around noon then?" But he said this to her mother, not to her. The jackass.

"I won't be available," Sierra said loudly even as Mom nodded and patted him on the arm.

Mom slid into the seat and Sierra glared at her, feeling peevish and fifteen and not caring because at least it was somewhere for her frustration to go. "I can't believe you."

"I know you don't like it, but until you talk it through, nothing is solved."

"We're not staying together. I'm sure of it. So, there's nothing to solve."

"Not staying together is fine. If that's your decision, Sierra, that's more than fine. Your father and I will support you in whatever way we can. But you have to know why you're making the decision first, or you're going to have a lot of regrets."

Sierra wanted to retort that she knew exactly why she was making the decision, but finding words for all that knowledge seemed impossible.

CARTER STOOD ON Jess's stoop, waiting impatiently for the genius duo to answer the door. When Cole did, his eyebrows rose in surprise.

"It's not working," Carter said flatly.

"What's not working?"

"Where's Jess?" Carter demanded, looking over Cole's shoulder.

"She's at work." Cole shifted to let Carter in. Carter didn't particularly want to go inside the old house. It had been his grandfather's when they'd been kids and Carter had never felt comfortable in it. It had been the only place in his entire life where Cole had been the favorite.

For years he'd convinced himself that wasn't why he didn't like it. He was better than petty jealousy, but standing in the kitchen now—decorated with Jess's feminine touch—he realized that's all it had been.

Petty jealousy.

"What's not working?" Cole asked, and Carter had to admit it was weird seeing his brother like a...man. Cole had taken off at eighteen and spent most of the next ten years far away from Marietta. Carter still thought of him as that surly teenager.

But he wasn't. He was another person entirely. Somehow it made it easier to talk to him, thinking of him like someone else. Not the brother he'd never had anything in common with, but a man with a certain amount of life experience, just like him.

"The trying-hard thing. Sierra isn't coming around at all."

Cole tilted his head, looking Carter over like he'd gone a little crazy. "Carter… It's been two days."

"Yes. Two days. I've talked to her both days and she still insists that divorce is the only answer." It was taking everything he was to not act frustrated in front of her. To appear calm and reasonable.

But touching her and having her move away was… He didn't want to endure that ever again.

Cole ran a hand over his short hair and continued to study Carter with that obnoxious *you've lost it* gaze. "How long were you and Sierra married? A year?"

"In a little over a month it'll be our anniversary, but we've been together over a year now."

"Okay, so in that year you ended up getting married and having your wife want to get divorced. I don't think you can fix that in two days. Forgiveness and acceptance and working through problems take time. Jess didn't exactly fall at my feet when she came and told me to come home to help Dad and the family. Or even when I actually did it."

Carter frowned. "But it didn't take *that* long. You've only been home a few months and you two are happy."

"We are, but we also weren't *married* back then. We were teenagers when we were together, and we're different people ten years later. And…relationships aren't math, Carter. They're messy and a lot complicated and different for everyone. You shouldn't be here telling me it's not working. You should be with Sierra figuring out how to make it work."

Carter really resented taking advice from his younger brother, but Cole was here and who else was Carter going to talk to? Lina was even younger and not happy with him. And he knew what his parents would say.

And that was his life. Without Sierra, his entire life was the McArthurs and the hospital. A supposed to, and yet it felt so empty and cold without her in it. When did that happen?

"Go talk to her," Carter urged. "Keep talking."

"She doesn't want to see me," Carter grumbled.

"Man, *what* did you do?"

"I didn't do anything!" Carter started pacing. It was so strange to have this anger clawing inside of him. He wasn't an angry guy, but it was growing. Every day. And it felt weirdly...good. It felt good to give in to this thing that wasn't rational. That wasn't *supposed to.*

Like Sierra. His not supposed to. He wanted more of that. More of all the good he'd gotten out of going against what he was *supposed* to do.

"You had to have done something."

Carter glared at his brother. "Well, whatever it was, I have no idea. And she won't tell me."

"Did you ask?"

"Yes, I did."

Cole sighed. "Look, I'm no marriage expert. I'm no anything expert, except how to wrestle a steer. But you can't fix it if you can't talk about what went wrong. If you don't know, you have to find out. And if she won't tell you... Well, I can't believe I'm about to say this, but that's a bit on her."

"Well, how do I change that?" Carter demanded.

"You don't. She has to want to."

"But how do I make her want to?" Cole was so big on wisdom and advice, why couldn't he give a straight damn answer?

"I don't think you can. I mean, in the way you're thinking. You can't go flip a magic switch or push the right button and she'll pop open and everything in your life will go back into order. You're looking for an answer. What you need is a solution."

"How is that different?"

"It just is."

"That doesn't make any sense. I should have waited for Jess."

"Maybe you should have. But, Carter, listen. I could be giving it to you all wrong. Who knows what the right answer is. There's only one thing I actually know, and that's whatever you do, however you handle this... Don't do it like Dad would. If you really love Sierra, make it be about that. Not McArthur bullshit. No manipulations. No trying to make someone do what *you* want them to do. That's what drives people away."

"That's what drove *you* away?"

Cole blew out a long breath. "It's not why I left, because that was Dad's machinations. I couldn't bend to his will, and I knew he'd give a lot more opportunities to Jess if I wasn't around. So I left. He didn't give me much of a choice, but all that—him trying to manipulate the situation, trying to make me what he wanted me to be, not what I'd be any good at being—that's what kept me away. I didn't want to be part of that. As an adult, I can see that he's not the evil monster I thought he was, but it doesn't mean he's the kind of man I want to be. It doesn't make him...good. It just makes him complicated."

"I never wanted Sierra to be anything but herself."

"Does *she* know that? Did you show her? Did you tell her? Jess and I are still working through this whole together thing. Figuring out how it's going to work. Figuring out what we need from each other. Half the time I wouldn't have a damn clue if she didn't tell me, and I'm sure it's vice versa. We weren't born to be mind readers."

"And that doesn't make you think you shouldn't be together?"

"No. We've been apart and we've been together. Life's better together. I'm better with her. I love her. That's the simple part. The hard part's putting in the work. And I think... Well, we were raised in the McArthur image. Be perfect. Don't let anyone see the cracks. That works in some areas, sure, but not when it comes to love. Love is all about letting people see the cracks."

Carter couldn't mask his look of disgust. Maybe that's how Cole felt. Or Jess, but it didn't make any sense to him. If you loved someone, why would you show them the worst of yourself?

"Jess is on twelves so she won't be home till late. I hate eating alone so if you want, you can come by for dinner. I'll have Lina over too."

"She doesn't want to see me," Carter noted.

Cole's mouth quirked. "That going to stop you?"

Dinner with just his siblings. It would be weird. Uncomfortable. Something he wasn't sure they'd ever really done. Definitely not as adults.

But the thought of spending another night alone in his house was worse than something a little weird. "Okay. I'll be here."

Chapter Six

"I'M NOT GOING."

Sierra looked at Lina's stubborn expression and fought the urge to say *good*. But as much as she felt some childish desire to have someone on her side, someone being just as upset with Carter as she was...Lina was *his* sister. And more, Sierra didn't want Carter alone and hurting. She just wanted her own hurting to stop.

"You should go," Sierra said firmly walking down the street in front of the hospital with Lina. They were both bundled up against the cold, and Lina would have to go finish her shift soon, but it felt good to get out of her mother's company for a little bit. Not because it was suffocating or disapproving as Sierra had anticipated, but because she was always five seconds from accidentally letting it slip she was pregnant.

If it was just Mom, she might have told her. But Mom would inevitably tell Dad and Sierra wasn't ready for that yet. Not when things felt okay between them. Dad *hated* Carter and blamed him for everything. It might not be true, but it felt good for her father to take her side for once. It felt good to coexist with her parents like... Well, almost like they were friends.

"He might be my brother, but I know whatever happened is all his fault."

Sierra tucked her chin into the big collar of her coat. She didn't want to talk about whose fault it was. That always confused her feelings, had her over-examining every second of the past few months and she'd so much rather move on.

No point dwelling in conflict. Love was supposed to be good and supportive and happy. Well, theirs hadn't turned out to be. The end. Obsessing over the story's details didn't change them any.

"Thank you."

"For what?" Lina demanded.

"For thinking it's all his fault."

"Well, it is, isn't it?"

"I'm sure your parents don't think so."

Lina rolled her eyes. "My parents can't see past their own eyeballs. It's funny, I used to think it was just because Carter must be so much better than us. Or, after Cole left, that Dad just ignored me because I was lacking in the penis department."

Sierra snorted out a laugh. Lina could always be counted on to say the frankest, funniest thing.

"But the thing is, I don't think it's about Carter really. Whatever warped thing they've got going on with him stems from all the...issues. Carter's been holed up ignoring everything and everyone the past few days, you know. Won't talk to anyone, even Mom. She's livid." Lina smiled.

"I'm sure he'll be back in no time."

"Probably," Lina agreed. "And I still think he's a jackass at fault but, if it helps you feel better, he isn't like himself at all."

Sierra thought about the two interactions she'd had with him today and yesterday. Lina was right. Even though he was still recognizably Carter, there were elements of him that were...off. The snippy comment about her carrying his baby—that wasn't Carter at all.

"I wish I could just skip ahead till this didn't hurt anymore," Sierra grumbled as they turned around and started to head back to the hospital.

"I said that about residency the other day. One of the older doctors gave me this big lecture about enjoying the moments, because they all have pros and cons, and when you move on there will be things you miss."

"I guess that's true."

"I think it's old-people bullshit."

Sierra snorted.

"I mean, how is life not going to be more fulfilling once you've got your own choices to make?"

"Well, life is full of choices you have to make that you don't want to. I'd rather not be divorcing your brother. I want it to work. It just doesn't. It's not a fun choice, even if it is mine."

Lina huffed. "Men are turds. I'm going to be alone forever."

Alone forever. It gave Sierra a little shudder to think of her life stretching before her *alone*. Except she wouldn't be. She had a baby coming, and she had her family.

Still she couldn't help picturing herself alone in bed night after night. No matter how hard she tried, she couldn't conjure up a fictional future partner who didn't have Carter's beautiful face.

But worse, so much worse, she had no problem picturing Carter with someone else. A doctor probably. A tall blonde doctor who would have eight million degrees, teach their baby French or something, and whisk everything Sierra had ever loved away—including this town.

What an awful, *awful* thought. And stupid. Because if Carter found someone else, she could too. Maybe not a doctor but a…a… Someone. Who did something.

"You okay?"

"Yeah, sure," Sierra forced herself to say. "You won't be alone forever. Someone will come along who'll make you swallow that sharp tongue of yours. You know, instead of run screaming in the opposite direction."

It was Lina's turn to snort. "I won't hold my breath. Better get back."

"Don't stay away from Carter on my account, okay? As much as I appreciate it, I don't need you to take sides. I want you to be happy, and Carter's your family. I don't hate him or anything. I'm frustrated and hurt and upset but I know... It's not like he purposefully did something to hurt me. We just didn't work. That's life, I guess. And you learn from your mistakes and move on to find the things that work." God, she prayed that was true.

Lina chewed on her lip for a few seconds. "I guess. But it's hard when you really want something to work and it doesn't. I really wanted you and Carter to work, and I know you did too."

Since Sierra felt like crying, she shrugged and looked away. "Yeah, well. I'll see you around. Maybe we can actually sit down somewhere warm and have lunch next time you have a day off."

"Yeah. Definitely."

"Bye, Lina."

"Bye."

Sierra huddled into her coat more, but instead of heading for her car, she decided to walk toward the Marietta River. Spring was still weeks if not months off and the wind was cold, but it was a sunny day and something about the brisk walk with Lina had felt refreshing.

Or maybe it was just the talking. The thinking about things instead of trying to ignore them. Maybe that's what Carter meant with all this five minutes business. Sure, he wanted to keep their marriage alive, but maybe instead of shying away Sierra needed to be strong enough to have those conversations. To create closure. For both of them.

Surely if she could find some closure she'd be able to picture a different future for herself than lonely nights.

Surely.

⁂

CARTER DIDN'T UNDERSTAND the point of suffering through dinner with his siblings. But then again, he didn't see much point in suffering through dinner alone.

He wasn't ready to suffer through dinner with his parents. He couldn't face them until he had some hope he and Sierra could work things out. No doubt they'd both heard the hospital rumors and he couldn't stand to think about their reactions.

The thought of listening to what his mother or father had to say about it was... No. He just couldn't do it. He'd fix things first. That was all there was to it.

So, here he was. Pulling up to where his brother lived, their grandfather's old house. Going to have dinner with the brother he'd pretty much only ever fought with.

His jaw practically dropped when he realized Lina's car was already parked there. Not just his brother, but the sister who currently thought he was a self-centered jackass.

Was he sure this was better than being alone?

Well, he was here anyway. He pushed his car into park and then stepped into the quickly falling dusk. It was bitterly cold, the wind whipping against his face making him wish he'd thought to put on a stocking cap even for the short walk to the door.

Still, he moved forward, knocking on the door and stepping inside when Cole opened it. The front door opened right up into the kitchen, the dining table right off the edge.

The room was warm if Lina's expression was not. She sat at the table, glaring at him.

"Almost ready if you want to sit down," Cole offered somewhat stiffly.

"Sure," Carter said, regretting this decision wholly as he walked toward the table. "Hi," he offered to Lina.

"Hi," she replied, and he braced himself for something snide as he settled himself into the chair across from her, but she didn't say anything else.

"First rule of family dinner," Cole announced, settling a bottle of cheap whiskey at the center of the table. "You say something asshole-ish, you take a shot."

"I don't drink," Lina retorted, her expression mulish.

"Then don't say something asshole-ish," Cole replied easily.

Carter could only stare at Cole. Carter still had this image of Cole as a young, angry teenager, even though he'd been back in Marietta these past few months. But Carter hadn't spent much time with him.

To see him, tall and broad and scarred from a decade of rodeo life, to hear him talk with the kind of assurance and candor Carter wasn't used to from anyone, it was disorienting. Now he was ordering Carter and Lina about and…

Well, Carter didn't know how to respond. There were so many things about the past few months that felt like he'd woken up from some decades-long coma. Everything around him foreign and different. His parentage. His siblings. His wife.

Cole shoved a large bowl of some muddy-looking chili in front of him, and then an identical bowl in front of Lina. He went back and got one for himself. "Drinks are on your own."

Lina rolled her eyes and got back up from the table. "Let me guess. Milk. Beer," she said pointing to Carter then Cole.

"Water," Cole said about the same time Carter said, "beer."

"Don't tell me things are actually changing around here just when I'm getting close to leaving," Lina muttered, rummaging through Cole's kitchen—well, Jess's kitchen. Cole and Jess's kitchen.

Yes, things were changing, and for the first time in his life Carter envied Lina a little bit. He should have gone away for his residency. He should have put his foot down. Done Doctors Without Borders or something—anything—for *him*, not Dad.

Who was not his father.

That still didn't make any sense to Carter, but it didn't cut him to the quick quite as painfully as it had at first. In fact, after the events of the past week it almost felt like relief.

Any failures he made didn't reflect on the man who couldn't abide failure.

Lina placed the drinks on the table and resettled herself. "So, what's the point of all this, Cole? I don't really think it's for fun."

"Not fun, exactly. But for the future. Our future."

"Is this some creepy business proposition? Are you going to try to sell me leggings?"

Cole's expression went puzzled. "What are leggings?" He shook his head. "Whatever. It's not business. It's life. The rodeo circuit is heating up and I won't be able to be gone for just weekends anymore. A good six months of being on the road lies ahead of me, and Jess will be with me some of the time but most of the time she'll be here. I don't want to leave her with a nest of surly, bickering McArthurs."

"Didn't worry you ten years ago," Lina pointed out.

"I'd make you take a shot for that except you're right. I thought I was doing the right thing, but it wasn't. But I'm not eighteen anymore and neither are you." He turned his gaze to Carter. "Or you. We're adults. I don't know about you two, but I have a future to build. I'm going to marry Jess once we're ready. We're going to have a family at some point. Here, in Marietta. Home. I need to know… I can't fix Mom and Dad. Maybe they don't even need fixing. I don't know. But if I'm going to build a family here, I want the McArthur name to mean something to my family, or for them. Not the way it means something to Dad. I want it to mean they have a family. Support, no matter what choices they make. Love. Security."

Carter blinked down at his dreary-looking chili. A family. He'd been so wrapped up in getting Sierra back, he'd focused more on the idea of pregnancy than *family*. Focused more on the science of it than the end result. Children. A child. There was going to be a living, breathing child. *His* child.

Cole wasn't even married or procreating and he was thinking about his future family. What he wanted for them.

And Carter was going to be a *father* in the rather near future. He needed to be thinking about these kinds of things too. His child as a being rather than a murky idea.

"I don't know how you're going to make that happen, Cole. We're all warped. We've always been warped," Lina said.

It matched Carter's own thoughts on the matter, but something about thinking about the future unlocked some other feeling inside of him. A kind of denial or refusal.

No, he didn't want this for his kids. Having to be perfect or thinking they were better only to reach their thirties and realize it was all a bunch of manipulative bullshit. It kept you apart and alone and…wrong, somehow. In ways you couldn't quite figure out.

No, he didn't want that for his kids. He wanted a bright, warm world for them and God knew Sierra would give that to the child, but he wanted to as well. He wanted to live in that warmth. The three of them.

"I'd rather be single forever than be like them," Lina muttered. "Don't know why it took so long to see it."

"I think they love each other in their warped way," Cole offered.

"Why do you think that?"

"Did you watch them when they announced Dad's diagnosis and Carter's... Well. They reached out. Held on to each other. Maybe they're not the best people, but maybe they're not the worst either. They're not monsters. Warped, yeah. Wrong, definitely. But they're...human too."

Lina looked incredibly dubious, but Carter figured Cole had a point. It wasn't one he could untangle or process right here in this instant, but there was something to them not being evil monsters, or perfect saints. Something about that messy gray area he'd always shied away from.

He didn't particularly want to dive into it now, but he didn't want to lose Sierra. He didn't want to be a crappy brother to his siblings, and he didn't want to be a man made out of the perfect McArthur image.

Not just because it was a lie, but because it wasn't worth upholding if it meant a life without the people he loved. Without being free to love them in other ways than he was used to.

For the first time in his entire life, he understood why Sierra had said she couldn't be a McArthur and be happy.

Now if he only knew how to convince her being a McArthur didn't have to mean that unhappiness anymore.

Chapter Seven

IT WAS TOO cold to be sitting on a bench in Crawford Park watching the icy Marietta River trickle idly in the sunlight.

Sierra lifted her face to the sun though. No matter the temperature, or more importantly, the windchill, she needed to get out more. Feel the sun on her face. Breathe the fresh air. She'd been shutting herself inside these past few months, letting everything fall in on itself.

She needed to throw open the windows and breathe fresh, new air into her brand-new start.

She opened her eyes at the sound of a car door and looked over to see Carter walking toward her.

She had to deal with the past before she could fully step into her fresh start. So, she'd agreed to meet him today. On her own terms. Where and when she wanted.

"A bit cold, isn't it? We could sit in the car or—"

"Let's walk," Sierra interrupted. She wanted to move. She was finding the more she got up and did things, the less puny and nauseous she felt.

"So, I guess you're feeling...well," he finished, kind of

lamely.

She side-eyed him as they walked along a little trail. He hadn't reacted to the baby news like she'd expected, that was for sure. "I have to say I'm surprised you haven't tried to doctor your way into this."

"It's all still surreal. Hard to believe. I probably would have though, if things were...normal. But I also know there's probably a few more weeks before they'll do a checkup, so I have time."

Sierra rolled her eyes. She should have known he had a plan, though she'd give him a tiny bit of credit for his honesty.

"I should be there. Not as a doctor, but as your husband and as the baby's father. I should be at all your appointments."

"But you're not going to be my husband, Carter. I need you to accept that. Time won't change my mind. Some magic fact you come up with won't change my mind. I have to make a new start."

"Why do you have to do that?"

"Why?" she spluttered. She couldn't believe the question. Did why matter when she'd made her decision? "Because. That's why."

"Shouldn't you be able to tell me why?" he asked, and there was an odd edge to his tone. One she didn't recognize.

"I can. Maybe I don't want to."

He shook his head. "That isn't right, and it isn't fair.

Maybe you think I should know or be able to understand through magic or whatever, but that isn't fair." He shoved his hands in his pockets and watched his feet as they walked. He opened his mouth, but didn't speak right away, almost as if he was struggling with something. "I'm human, Sierra."

She wanted to be angry at that simple statement of fact. As if she expected him to be perfect and godlike. She wasn't his father. She had never, ever had those kinds of expectations of him. In fact, she'd always wished he'd be a little less perfect so she didn't feel so dumb in comparison.

But in the sunshine of a winter afternoon, she realized *he* expected himself to be that perfect, inhuman robot. And admitting he was only human was something of a step.

Some little bubble of hope took hold of her fast and hard, but she had to pop it. Reality was that no matter what steps he took or what he realized, there was no positive future for them together. They'd had their shot. It hadn't worked. She had to be firm in that.

She couldn't wake up suspecting he didn't love her again. She couldn't live in a constant cycle of knowing she wasn't enough while he turned away from her, and that felt inevitable. If it happened so easily, so early in their marriage, how could it not happen again?

"Fine. If you must know, I want a new start because I was miserable and making myself more so. A marriage isn't two people barely talking or hardly seeing each other. And it's…" She struggled to find the right word. One that fit but didn't pain her to admit. "It's not fun to shrink to take up less and less space. I won't do it anymore."

"What if I don't want you to do it anymore either? What if I wanted you to take up more space?"

You wouldn't let me. Part of her wanted to say it. To lay it all out there. The way he'd shut her out and down, but she couldn't get her lips to work that way. The thought of baring her soul filled her with such body-numbing fear she could barely suck in a breath.

She'd spent most of her teenage years embracing her weaknesses so it didn't hurt when her father chided her for them. But for some reason when it came to Carter, she'd been afraid to let him see any of them. At least the ones that would kill her to have him criticize.

She could handle someone calling her flighty or overdramatic. She knew she was those things, and she didn't see much point in being different. But she didn't want Carter to see how soft her heart was, how much it hurt when he acted as though she didn't even exist. How it made her feel as worthless as she always secretly suspected she was.

She wanted to be stronger than all that. Tougher. Tough and hard was the only way to get through life. Dad had tried to impart that on all of them.

Now she'd spent the past few days under her father's roof and seen a softer side to the gruff, hardworking man she'd cast as the villain in her teenage rebellions. But something in her adult life had made her realize even if he'd gone about it the wrong way, he'd been trying to teach them how to survive a tough world.

She should have listened better. Maybe her heart wouldn't be so bruised and bloody.

"The five minutes doesn't count if it's silent," Carter said gently.

"The talking is your idea."

"I guess I could tell you about my dinner companions last night."

She felt her mouth curve in spite of herself. It was so cute when he thought he was sneaky or had some piece of information she didn't. He was always wrong because usually he was so wrapped up in something or other he hadn't noticed it the first time around.

"Absent-minded professor," she murmured.

"You haven't called me that in... Well, I think since before we got married."

Oof. She didn't want to dive into that well of hurt. The way things had changed once they'd gotten married. Once she'd been McArthurized. So, she wouldn't. "You had dinner with Cole and Lina."

"How'd you know that?" he asked, sounding slightly incredulous, which helped take her mind off all that hurt.

"Lina and I hung out a bit yesterday on her break. She said she wasn't going to go though, so that was just a guess on my part."

"I was glad she did."

"Kaitlin and I have been getting along," Sierra said, and then immediately regretted it. They weren't here to talk like they were a happy married couple on a walk.

"Really? How is Kaitlin? I haven't seen her much since... Well."

"Since she got knocked up and married Beckett Larson, thus ending her decades-long crush on you?"

"She did not have a crush on me."

"Oh, please. She was desperately in love with you."

He scoffed, and it was a little odd, Sierra realized in retrospect, that she'd never really talked with Carter about how stupid Kaitlin used to be over him.

"That isn't true, is it?" he asked, as if figuring out she was serious.

"God's honest truth."

He stopped mid stride and turned to her, eyes wide, mouth open. "*That's* why you came over to me at that party when we met."

Again she had to fight the urge to smile. "Why?"

"To piss off your sister."

"She wasn't there."

"No, but... You never would have given me the time of day if you weren't trying to do something. Stick it to your sister is as good an answer as any." He sounded...awed, taken aback.

She wanted to back away from all this, *run* away from where it all began. She didn't want to rehash, or worse, feel it all over again. But she'd decided to embrace this whole five minutes thing because she wanted to find closure. She wanted to walk away with no regrets, so her fresh start really was fresh.

"Yes, I came over to you at the party because I knew Kaitlin was all hung up on you and would get all pissy if I said I'd flirted with you, especially on New Year's Eve." She wasn't exactly proud of herself, but she'd been bored and restless and it had been something to do.

"But you married me. I assume you didn't do *that* to piss Kaitlin off."

If only.

SIERRA STARTED WALKING again and Carter had no choice but to follow. "I know you didn't," he said, because even though he did know that, her silence was…perplexing.

"No," she finally admitted.

The wind was icy and he wanted to bundle her up and put her somewhere warm, but she would bristle at that and only stay out in the cold longer.

See? He wasn't completely clueless. He understood *some* things about her.

"Funny thing is I thought I'd go over, flirt with the golden-boy doctor, get him a little riled up then disappear. Have a big laugh with my friends, make Kaitlin seethe with jealousy."

"You didn't though."

"No. The golden boy who I thought would be interested in slumming it for approximately two seconds, ten if I showed enough cleavage..." She sighed heavily and unexpectedly whirled around, immediately striding back toward where their cars were parked.

He had quite a few inches on her, so it was easy to catch up.

"You were *nice*," she said, sounding very close to disgusted, which of course made no sense to him. Wasn't nice good?

"You weren't disdainful of the bad girl smiling up at you. You didn't treat me like you knew my nickname in high school was Sierra Do-her. You just talked to me like I was some adult, whole person separate from my reputation or my family or how far out of your league I was."

"Sierra...Do-her?"

"You're missing the point."

"No. I got the point, but I'm hung up on the nickname. Did people really call you that?"

Sierra shrugged jerkily. "Whatever. I wasn't exactly picky or discreet. That was kind of the point."

"We didn't run in the same circles." Maybe it was strange to comment on, but he'd had a certain tunnel vision after he'd met her at that party. He hadn't thought about much beyond how she made him feel. He'd thought about the person in front of him. If he'd known anything about Sierra before that moment it had been that she and the Shullers existed. His mother had made sure to tell him she was 'wild' a few times, but Carter hadn't paid much attention to that. Her past was a mystery, because all that had mattered to him was *her*.

The thought of any asshole daring to touch her then call her that about made him rage right there, but he supposed that was beside the point. Still, it clawed at him like this new anger he always seemed to be carrying around.

"I mean, even without our age difference, yes, different circles. I didn't think it mattered, but maybe it does."

"It doesn't," he said automatically, firmly. He'd never believed that was what led them here.

"Carter." She heaved out a sigh that puffed into a cloud against the cold air around them. She came to a stop and wrapped her arms around herself. "I know you want that to be true, but I've had to come to the hard conclusion that the things we want to be true and the things that *are* true don't match up. We can't *make* the world do what we want."

He kept his mouth shut if only because he knew whatever argument he mounted would be met with her immediately dismissing it as his ego.

But he'd made everything in his life work except this, why shouldn't he have a little ego? Why shouldn't he believe this—the most important decision in his life—was right and good and this horrible blip was *fixable*?

For some reason, he remembered what Cole had said last night. Love was letting people see the cracks.

He inwardly shuddered at the idea. Maybe that worked for Cole and Jess, but Carter couldn't take it on board. But he could…modify it, for his own purposes. Maybe instead of showing her the cracks, the weakness, he should show her the strength. Why he was here, fighting for their marriage even though she was trying to walk away.

"You didn't ask why I talked to you when you came up to me at the party. Why I was nice."

"I don't need to ask. That's who you are, but sometimes you let *them* take it away, dim that goodness inside of you. You don't believe in it enough, and I can't believe in it for the both of us."

That felt like an arrow piercing too close to the truth. That weakness. He had to shield it.

"I talked to you, this woman too young and wild for the likes of me, the man who'd only ever associated with women my family would approve of, because you looked at me, flashed that smile I knew meant you wanted nothing but trouble, and my foundation shook. My rock-solid foundation that had never once, in my whole life, ever even trembled. It shook for you and I didn't want it to stop."

He expected her to say that didn't matter too, but she stood there instead, looking a little shaken herself.

So, he pressed his advantage and stepped closer with every word. "You damn well *sparkled* with life, and it was like nothing in my life. Nothing I'd ever seen. Not that close. Not that *right*." Her big brown eyes stared up at him and she swallowed, visibly. Audibly.

He reached out to touch her face, much like he had yesterday, because God it had been so long since he'd touched her right. The way she should be touched. Soft and reverent and his.

She didn't pull away like she had in the car. She inhaled shakily, and opened her mouth to say something, but he swept his thumb across her jawline like he knew she liked. No words escaped her throat, just a little squeaking sound that had something like power rushing through him, strong and bold.

Her eyes fluttered closed like they always did when he let his fingers trace slowly down the side of her neck, the most featherlight of touches.

He should have tried this before. Should have found this as solace in all that horrible darkness before. Her. Her softness. The way she responded to him. Maybe they wouldn't be here if he'd only—

But he hadn't. He only had now, and he'd use whatever he could to make this work.

He slid his hand around her neck, cupping the soft skin and silky strands of hair and pulling her closer.

"Carter…" But she said it on a whisper, and though he drew her nearer without saying a word, she didn't protest.

So he touched his mouth to hers, light at first. Simple.

Like their very first kiss under the stars after talking half the night away at that stupid party. And just like that night, she melted against him and he took more than he should have, drugged by the softness of her lips, the velvet of her tongue when it touched his. That bright pop of something bigger than chemistry or liking each other.

Like they were made from the stars that first night, shaped to belong together, to be each other's. That kiss and this one sealed that fate. Forever. He'd known then. He knew now. They belonged together.

She had to know it too. She *had* to.

But as he pulled away, his blood pumping, his heart racing, and everything inside of him whispering *Sierra,* it didn't matter that her eyes were glittering, or her cheeks were flushed from more than the cold. He knew in a horrible instant that the kiss wasn't a real acquiescence from her.

She stepped back. "I don't deny this—attraction. We've always had that," she said. Even though her voice was shaky and she was stepping away she seemed so…certain. Strong. "I don't even deny that we care about each other."

"What else matters?" he demanded, frustration leaking through.

"I'm not happy, Carter. You're not happy. We don't make each other happy."

"Nothing would have made me happy in the past few months. You don't know what it's like to find out your entire world view, self-view, *life view* is built on a lie."

"No, I don't. But why wasn't *I* a part of any of those views?"

It took him a good few seconds to actually feel that blow. To exhale the breath he'd taken as she'd said the words. It was too…true. Lina had said he only cared about himself and she was right. She was truly right. He'd absorbed his father's news and kept it all to himself, only thought of how it affected him.

He'd kept Sierra out of it, but she was wrong that it meant they should be over. It was one mistake. One wrong way of looking at things. It had been about cushioning the hurt, saving her from the pain. It hadn't been about not loving her.

So, he had made a mistake, yes, but he could fix it. Somehow.

"I don't want to talk about this anymore," she said, her voice scratchy as she turned and began walking toward her car. "Your five minutes are up."

"I love you, Sierra." Because it was all he had. The simplest truth he knew. He needed it to be enough for her, even knowing it wouldn't be.

"I love you too," she replied, pausing at her car door, but Carter knew she wasn't giving him what he wanted.

"But I don't want you," she continued. She got in her car, slammed the door shut, and Carter could only stand there. He didn't just feel sliced open, he felt as though all his organs were spilling out of him and he was nothing but an empty shell.

But her car didn't start or move. He had a fleeting moment of hoping she planned to get back out, take the words back, but then he realized she was moving around, punching the steering wheel.

Her car wouldn't start.

Carter glanced up at the sky, promised himself he'd believe in divine intervention if this worked, and he grinned.

Chapter Eight

SHE WANTED TO scream, but Carter had already caught sight of her punching the steering wheel and apparently thought it was quite hilarious based on that grin that skittered through her like light.

Oh, it had been so long since she'd seen him smile, really smile, and it felt like summer in the midst of all this winter. But nothing was hilarious after that kiss. Because no matter how she repeated what she'd told him in her head:

Of course we're attracted.

Of course we love each other.

That kiss reminded her so much of their first she could hardly shake off the need to run right back to him. She had never, ever expected to fall head over heels for Carter McArthur. *Doctor* Carter McArthur. She'd always been aware she was a bad girl—not exactly from the wrong side of the tracks, but certainly not from the McArthur side.

She'd never been like Kaitlin. Never tried to be good or responsible. She'd done what she wanted because it had been clear after all the arguing Dad and Luke had done that Dad would find fault either way.

But she'd fallen hard and fast for Carter and ignored that little niggling voice that had always told her she'd never be good enough for him. But it had come back and with a vengeance, hadn't it? The past few months had been nothing about *knowing* she wasn't good enough for him. Not good enough to be confided in. Not good enough to accept comfort from. Not good enough to trust.

Giving in to this now would only repeat the last year on a cycle. Maybe they'd be happy for a bit, but that McArthur world where he and they were the center and she didn't factor into any of his 'life views'... It would all come back.

She'd tried the love route, and it hadn't made either of them happy.

For some reason she thought of Kaitlin and Beckett, who were one of the most demonstratively in love couples she knew. Sierra knew Kaitlin had never planned on falling for their brother's bad boy of a best friend, and she knew that Kaitlin's unplanned pregnancy had played a part.

But they so clearly loved each other. What sense did that make?

Carter tapped on the window and she scowled at him.

"Go away." Childish? Yes, but she'd spent five minutes being very adult and talking about things that hurt like hell and she was done with it.

He motioned for her to open the door. There really wasn't another choice. She couldn't freeze in her car for another twenty minutes or however long it would take to find someone free to come pick her up and take her home.

"I'll drive you home."

"No, I'll call my dad. But I'll sit in your car with the heater on while we wait. Silently, of course. If you can agree." She could be adult if she had to be.

"Sierra. Let me drive you home. I promise, I won't say a word."

If he was anyone else, she wouldn't have believed that promise, but even in all this...weirdness, Carter didn't lie. Oh, he might go off into his own little world, might shut her out, might turn into someone else completely and then slowly start to morph back into the man she knew, but he didn't lie.

She had to remember not to trust that morphing. It was temporary now just like it had been before. The next bad-news thing and he'd behave the same way. There was no hope. She couldn't allow herself to have any.

"Fine," she agreed, because if he had to be silent, she could be home and crawl into bed in the next fifteen minutes. God, she was tired.

She got out of her car and followed him to his. True to his word, he didn't talk. They simply buckled, he started the car, and then he started driving.

Sierra yawned. She'd take a nap when she got home. Pregnant women got to have naps without guilt. Damn straight. She yawned again. She'd just close her eyes until she got home. It would make it so much easier to ignore him, that was for sure.

She had no idea how much later she awoke with a start. The sun seemed unbearably bright. The car wasn't moving, but she was in it, still buckled. She blinked and looked over at Carter in the driver's seat. He was reading something on his phone.

"What..." But before she could finish that sentence her gaze drifted to what lay outside the window.

It was not her parents' house. It was not Marietta. It was an unbelievable view of mountains and a valley below, the sun setting into it and shining directly at her. She was almost awed, until she realized how far away from her destination they were. How *late* it was.

She screeched. "Where the hell did you take me?"

Carter only smiled calmly, maneuvering so he could slide his phone into his back pocket. "Beautiful, isn't it? I can't believe we've never found time to come up here. My fault, I know."

She gaped at him. Was this a dream? Had he sustained a head injury? Had *she*?

But it all made a horrible kind of sense. "Your parents' cabin." Outside Marietta, closer to damn Yellowstone. Was he *insane*? "Are you insane?" she demanded. No use only thinking it.

"*Insane* isn't the word I'd use. But we could use some time alone. Together. Let's get inside. I've wasted an awful lot of gas sitting here letting you sleep. Be a shame to not be able to leave when we're ready because we ran out of gas."

"I'm ready. I'm ready right now! I can't believe you did this. I can't believe…" She had no words for all the things she couldn't believe. Carter had been devious. He'd *tricked* her. Carter. The man who didn't even like practical jokes because they were too close to a lie.

She took a deep breath, gathering together all her strength and pride and…whatever you called what was going to get you through a horrible thing. Grit, maybe. Yeah, she liked that. She wanted to have *grit*.

"Take me home. Now," she ordered, giving him a look Mrs. McArthur was forever giving her. Disdainful and disgusted.

"Wouldn't be smart to drive these icy roads in the dark," Carter replied as if they were having a calm, *sane* conversation. "Especially when we're so low on gas. Have to spend the night."

He said it so cheerfully she wanted to junk-punch him. "I'm not spending the night with you here. I refuse." She grabbed her purse and started pawing through for her phone. "I'll call someone to pick me up."

"And have them brave the icy roads in the dark?" he asked casually. Not even disapprovingly. Just a simple, non-threatening question.

Damn him. *Damn. Him.* "I will make you pay for this. In ways you can't even fathom."

"Trust me, I spent plenty of time fathoming on my way

up here. I even turned around once. But as mad as you are, as mad as you're going to be, the only thing that's going to solve this problem is time together."

"No. The only thing that's going to solve this problem is div—"

He reached out and put his hand on her stomach out of nowhere. Just his big hand on her still-flat stomach, and she nearly burst into tears in that second. Pregnancy felt like such a disconnected experience this early. She *knew* there was something in there, but it was hard to really wrap her head around the reality of it.

Carter's hand on her stomach made it feel impossibly real. It made the connection between them a tangible thing. No matter how she told herself to be strong, to be sure, she was *torn*.

Couldn't she put up with hard times and him shutting himself away if it meant they got to do this together?

She looked up at him, his blue gaze on her stomach before it slowly lifted to hers.

She was so close to crying, to giving in. "I can't do this," she whispered. "I can't keep doing this, Carter. You have to stop."

His gaze was so solemn, so *caring*. It nearly undid her completely.

"Let's go inside and get you something to eat," he said, acknowledging nothing at all.

She wanted to argue, but what other choice did she have?

She *was* hungry, and feeling nauseous, and still fuzzy from sleep.

If they went inside, he'd take his hand off her stomach and she could remember that she'd made a decision. The right decision, and second thoughts and doubts were only weakness talking.

God, she really hoped she could remember that.

CARTER DEPOSITED SIERRA on the expensive leather couch Mom had bought in one of her redecorating frenzies. Carter had never figured the furniture in the family cabin made much of a difference when there were big picture windows showing a breathtaking view of the mountains and valley below.

Who cared what the indoors looked like?

He'd already been inside to turn the heat up and whatnot while Sierra had been sleeping, so it was nice and warm, but he grabbed one of the throw blankets from the sleek, modern cabinet that dominated the side wall anyway.

He draped it over Sierra's lap, not missing the angry glare she kept focused on him.

He knew she'd be angry for taking her anywhere but home, and maybe he should feel guilty about that. But he wasn't. She kept walking away just when they were getting somewhere. Maybe he shouldn't be so impatient after three days, but in reality it had been something like months.

His fault, yes, but that just meant it was his responsibility to fix things. So, he would.

"Soup? Frozen pizza? I can make some hot chocolate."

She groaned from over on the couch. "Just one. Whichever one. But just one, please."

"It's a little early to be having morning sickness," he offered, looking over his shoulder at her.

She was typing angrily onto her phone. "Why don't you crawl inside my stomach and tell it that?"

Carter opened a cabinet and grabbed two cans of chicken noodle soup. She was likely texting her parents. Or maybe Lina. "Right. Well. Just so you know, I told your parents you wouldn't be home."

When there was nothing but a vibrating silence, Carter glanced away from his soup preparations to her spot on the couch.

Her mouth was hanging open and she stared at him like he was some kind of psychopath.

"I didn't want them to worry," he explained, focusing back on the task of dumping soup into a pot on the stove. "I knew they would worry, considering they likely knew you'd been with me and it was only supposed to be for a brief meeting. So, I called your mom and told her we were going away for a day or two to try and work things out."

"A day or..." She inhaled deeply as if trying to calm herself. "Is this high-handed bullshit supposed to be winning me over?" she demanded.

"No, it's supposed to be giving me a chance." He frowned at the soup. "All I want is a chance."

She didn't have anything to say to that, so he focused on getting bowls and rounding up crackers. He was lucky Mom and Dad had been here last weekend and one of their hospital friends was coming up next so they weren't bare bones on the necessities. Too bad he hadn't had a chance to buy a carton of milk. Sierra should probably be drinking milk.

No doubt her parents were taking good care of her though, except... He filled the bowls and walked them to the little glass table he hated eating at, but it was too cold to eat outside. "Have you told your parents?" he asked.

"Told them what? I think they figured out the whole I'm leaving you thing."

"That we're pregnant."

He imagined the snort of derision she gave him was over the word *we're* but that wasn't about to stop him from considering this *their* pregnancy even if he didn't have to do any of the hard parts.

"I haven't told them. I..." She placed her hands over her stomach. "It's so early. It feels... I don't want to start telling people until it feels more certain. More possible."

Carter nodded. "I haven't told anyone either, and I won't until you're ready. But I still want to come to your first appointment."

"Right because the entire medical community wouldn't spread that around like wildfire. Carter and Sierra McArthur were in her OBGYN's office together! I think we know what that means. And I hear they're divorcing. The elder Dr. McArthur will be so thrilled to be rid of that trash."

"He doesn't think you're trash, and what's more important, I don't."

"Is it more important when you respect him as much as you do?"

A hard question to untangle because he didn't respect his father, or non-father, the way he had. He wasn't sure it had ever been respect, exactly. Awe. Yes. He'd wanted people to react to him like they reacted to Gerald. Was that respect? Were respecting him and loving her mutually exclusive?

"Come eat," he said instead of figuring that all out. His father didn't have anything to do with this. This was about him and Sierra.

She glared up at him, though there was something other than anger in her expression. He couldn't read it—reading expressions was not his strong suit—but even beyond that he thought she was trying very hard to hide whatever it was.

"You can't keep me here forever," she said, not making a move to get off the couch.

"No, I have tomorrow off work, but then I'll have to be back at the hospital."

She rolled her eyes, flinging the blanket off her lap and getting to her feet. "Of course."

"Was I working too much? Is that it? Getting too wrapped up in the hospital? Because that's an easy fix, Sierra."

"No, that wasn't it, jackass. I wasn't afraid to ask you to stay home. I'm not afraid to ask for what I want."

He mulled that over in his head. He'd always thought that true. Sierra was so forthright and, well, volatile at times, he'd always figured if something was wrong, if she needed something, she'd voice it.

But clearly that wasn't true, no matter what she said about herself. Because there was something he'd done or something she'd needed that he hadn't given her, something that was making her *unhappy*—miserable was the word she'd used—and she refused to tell him what it was.

She sat down to the soup and sighed, but she started to eat so he did the same. He watched her while he did. She didn't look up at him. Not once. She was focused on the soup.

The thing was, he'd been in a kind of fugue state almost these past few months. They'd barely interacted and that was all on him. In trying to fix things, in wanting her to explain what went wrong, he wasn't ignoring the fact he'd made some grave mistakes. But he was trying to understand why it had gotten so bad.

Sitting across from her didn't feel wrong. He hadn't suddenly woken up to find a stranger. She was the same as she ever was. The woman he loved with all of his being. He'd treated her wrong, yes, but that hadn't meant he didn't feel the same.

In fact, it wasn't her at all. *He* had changed some. He was a little different. He wasn't sure why, maybe finding out his life had been based on a lie made him pay a little more attention to the world around him, to more than McArthurs and what he was supposed to do. Even more attention to the woman who'd been his not supposed to—that he'd promised to love and cherish forever anyway.

She loved him. She'd said so herself. But something was missing, and she didn't want to fight for it. She didn't want to dissect it and figure out what it was.

There was a kind of pattern in that. Subtle, definitely, because Sierra always seemed so confident. She'd never withered under his mother's cruelties. She'd oftentimes given right back. Carter had assumed it was because she was secure and didn't care what his mother thought, which had made it easy not to intervene.

But Sierra had a habit of giving up on hard things she actually wanted. He hadn't noticed it over the past few months, but there was a pattern in their year together. An art scholarship he'd urged her to apply for—she'd gotten halfway through the application then given up on it before they'd been married. She'd quit helping her sister out with a project at the florist shop where Kaitlin worked when they'd bickered too much last summer.

He'd known all those things separately, but he'd never put them together. Doing so now was painful. Not just because he's missed it before, but because he saw a hint of vulnerability in the woman he'd seen as strong and capable and a storm no one dare cross.

But she needed crossing. She needed more from him.

Because he wasn't letting her walk away from this when he knew she loved him, when he knew she was afraid of reaching out for good things.

They just had to find some better way to communicate these things. Some way to talk that gave her the freedom to either realize it about herself or be willing to acknowledge it or whatever it was that was holding her back.

"I had this friend in college," he began, trying to sound casual. "English wasn't his first language, though he was a proficient enough speaker. Still, sometimes he'd really struggle with a word or concept. That reminds me of us sometimes. Like we're speaking different languages."

"Gee, sounds like a perfect couple. We should totally stay married and keep making each other miserable!"

It shouldn't be funny, but he'd always found Sierra's somewhat scathing sense of humor just that. Even in the darkest of circumstances. But the smile died slowly because *she* had never made him miserable. "If people never tried to understand each other, we'd be awfully isolated and lonely."

She scowled into her soup. "I'm familiar with those feelings," she muttered.

"So, maybe we should try to understand each other. Maybe we should talk about that instead of run away from it."

Chapter Nine

HAVING HOPE SUCKED, and Sierra wanted to hurt Carter for trying to infuse it back into her. Hope only ever made people miserable. Dad had hoped he'd make enough money to be comfortable and not have to work so hard. Mom had hoped Dad wouldn't take all the stress of trying to make ends meet on himself. Luke had hoped Dad would be kinder, gentler about his dyslexia. Kaitlin had hoped Carter would notice her and marry her.

Maybe Mom and Dad had found a little peace with their kids out of the house, and Luke and Dad's antagonism had cooled. Maybe Kaitlin had found a husband she loved after Sierra had married the man of her sister's dreams. Maybe, *maybe*, it all worked out, but that didn't mean hope was safe.

First you got crushed to bits.

She'd had her own hopes. Silly childish hopes dashed by her father's heavy practicality and then nasty rumors and stupid middle school stuff that had followed her no matter where she went or how.

So she'd learned to embrace it. All of it. Fling herself into the middle of all that failure.

Until Carter had smiled at her at that party, and she'd had the blinding, idiotic belief maybe she wasn't as much of a disaster case as she'd always considered herself. If the upstanding, honest, gorgeous Dr. Carter McArthur could look at her like she dazzled him, then, well.

"We should talk, Sierra. Really talk. Not in five-minute snippets. Not trading smart remarks back and forth. An honest conversation. *That's* why I brought you here. It isn't so sinister, is it? To want to work out where I went wrong."

She took a few spoonfuls of soup, trying to let that spark of temper outweigh all the sadness inside of her. "Why and what for? It's just done. No post-mortem or research paper on the subject needed."

"I don't get why you're acting like a conversation is some sort of attack on you," he said, and with each word his frustration and anger started to become more prominent, which wasn't like him at all. "I don't understand your determination this is just over when we haven't even tried."

"I tried," she whispered, because as much as she wanted to be angry it just felt awful and devastating to admit this. He wanted all these admissions from her that only made her look weak and worthless, and no matter that she might be, she didn't want him to see it. She couldn't stand *watching* him see it.

If he'd tried even a month ago, she might have been soft enough to give in, but she'd given him too much time and too much hope. She couldn't jump into that old belief this part of her life would be different. Because it would lead her here, over and over again.

"Try now," he said, and it was almost imploring, but there was such ego there. That he could just command her to try again and she would when he'd had months upon months.

She pushed back from the table. She could tell him no. Tell him she wasn't doing this, but she'd been doing that for all these days since he'd finally decided she was worth fighting for.

No, not her, because if it had been about her he would have fought *before* she'd delivered those papers. He was simply fighting now because the only other outcome was divorce and that would shame him. Or maybe he was only fighting now because of the baby. Either way, it wasn't enough.

"Where are you going?" he asked as she started down the hallway, hoping to find a bedroom or somewhere she could lock herself in a room and sleep until tomorrow.

"Sierra."

She ignored him and opened the first door she came to. It was a bathroom, so she pressed on.

"Stop."

She considered flipping him off, but in the end ignoring him worked better. She opened the next door and there was a giant bed with a wall made up almost entirely of windows like in the living room. Perfect. It was dark but she could see the moon. Comforting, and it was early enough she could get a good amount of sleep before the sun came back up.

She stepped inside and then moved to close the door, but Carter slapped his hand on it to keep it from closing. His eyes glittered with fury and his mouth was a sharp, painful slash on that usually calm face.

It was so strange to see him furious she could only stare at him. Part of her wanted to reach out and touch him to see if it was real.

"Damn it, Sierra," he growled. "You will listen to me. You will answer me. I deserve that much."

Deserve. That word infuriated her right back. "For what?"

"My God." He let his hand fall from the door and raked his fingers through his hair. "I don't know, maybe love?"

"Fine. *Fine*." He wasn't going to let this go. Stubborn man. She often didn't recognize it because he didn't dress it up in stomping displays, but he *was* stubborn. Sometimes even more than her. "Fine, you want me to try now. Now?" She whirled away from him and stalked toward the window, wishing she could find something to hold on to. Something to keep her focused and from blurting out all the pain inside of her.

"Yes, I do."

"I spent months having you look through me." God, that hurt to say, to admit. To tell him she'd seen how little she meant, to watch him see how much it had hurt her. "And that was after you kept this giant secret from me." She tried to straighten her shoulders, firm her expression, but tears started to fall and her voice croaked. "No matter what I did, you were a blank wall. *I tried* through all of that while I didn't matter to you. You're ready to try something like six months too late, Carter."

"I was... I know I didn't treat you right." He reached out and touched her shoulder. "I am sorry, but I was... I wasn't myself."

She whirled away from his touch, happy to have some anger to infuse this bone-crushing sadness. "That's it? You weren't yourself. You're sorry."

"I can't go back and change it."

"No. You can't. And I won't go back and change my mind about divorce."

"Because I was going through a rough time and didn't pay attention to you?"

She closed her eyes against the stab of pain. That right there was exactly what she'd been afraid of. That he'd belittle what she felt. Act like she was the problem for needing more from him.

And maybe she was.

"I want to go to bed, Carter."

"We are not done discussing this. If this is all it is—"

"All right." If she couldn't run away, she'd just have to get mean. "You want to *discuss* things. Let's talk about how your father told you he wasn't actually your father and you let me walk into a family meeting to get ambushed by that information." She forced herself to look at him even though there were tears on her cheeks.

He did that thing she'd always hated, even when she'd been so besotted with him she overlooked everything. He got very stiff, and his expression went blank. He sort of raised his chin as if he were a king surveying his manor.

It was a very *Dr. McArthur* look.

"Is that what this is really about? That meeting?"

"So, to be clear, in your version of a conversation, I ask a question and you counter with one of your own?"

He pressed his lips together, some frustration slipping through that cool McArthur detachment he'd surrounded himself with. Good. She wanted to frustrate him. She wanted to make him mad—even madder than he'd been when she'd ignored him.

She wanted him so furious he'd realize it wasn't worth it. *She* wasn't worth it.

"I couldn't…" Something closer to confusion drew his eyebrows together. "It wasn't you, Sierra. I couldn't tell anyone. I still haven't…"

"Still haven't what?" she demanded when he just stuttered and looked so miserable she wanted to cross to him.

"I haven't *said* it. Those words. Not…to anyone."

"What words?"

"I am not…" He took a deep breath, raked his fingers through his hair one more time, and when he spoke his voice was little more than a whisper. "I am not Gerald McArthur's son."

CARTER HAD SAID it once, drunk as a skunk, alone in his house. To say it here, in this cabin, in front of Sierra...

It was horrible. Painful. He felt like crying, and he wasn't drunk this time so there was no good excuse for the stinging in his eyes.

But there was something else too. A load lifted off his shoulders. A certain soaring...

Freedom.

"I am not Gerald McArthur's son," he repeated. Stronger this time. "I am not a McArthur."

He glanced over at her, where she stood staring at him as if he'd lost his mind. Maybe he had. Because Cole's words about showing the cracks were revolving around in his head.

Nothing he was doing was getting through to her. Not telling her he loved her, not remembering why they'd fallen for each other or revisiting old memories. Not even that kiss by the river.

But she was looking at him right now as he said the hardest words he'd ever had to say. Watching him as he felt like he was falling apart from the inside out.

She wasn't walking away or saying anything terrible to him. She was standing there, as if waiting for more.

It scared him to his soul, the thought of letting it all out, but he knew this little stunt he'd pulled in getting her here meant everything was now or never. Five minutes wasn't going to last past this. This really was his last chance to get through to her.

And if it failed, he at least got to blame Cole for bad advice.

"You know how much I looked up to my father."

"Your father's an ass."

Maybe Carter shouldn't have been, but he was surprised at her vehemence. He'd known her feelings about his family, but she tended to not voice it. He'd always thought that was considerate of her since he had a complicated but necessary relationship with them.

"We should have dealt with that."

"What? Your father being an ass?"

"Yes. I shouldn't have ignored it. I shouldn't have ignored the way they treated you and you shouldn't have told me it didn't matter when it did."

"It *didn't* matter," she said fiercely.

But he... He just didn't believe her. "What else have you lied to me about?"

"What?" she replied, outrage written all over her face and in her fists clenching. But he couldn't be worried about offending her when it was so true. "I am not *lying*."

"What else have you said didn't matter or was fine when it clearly wasn't? My family. My silence. What else?"

"Nothing. I don't know what you're talking about. You're just... You're just making things up now."

He moved then, because it downright infuriated him she could lie like that. Right to his face. Not just now, but for this whole time. Lied and told him everything was fine when it wasn't.

Maybe he should have known. He could cop to that. But she shouldn't have lied. They were both wrong here, and they both had to fight to fix it. He'd go first, but he needed her to come with him.

She backed away from him as he walked toward her. She kept stepping backward right up until she hit the wall with a little *oof*. But he didn't stop. He walked until they were leg to leg, looking down at her wide, uncertain eyes.

"What. Else?" His teeth and fists were clenched because he didn't want to yell. He didn't want to *scare* her. But he wanted...something.

"Go away," she said, giving him an ineffective shove—both because it was barely even a nudge and because he was so locked in place likely nothing would knock him over.

"Tell me what else you lied to me about."

"I didn't lie. Sometimes... Sometimes a person keeps things to themselves out of self-preservation, Carter. And it doesn't have anything to do with you, so knock it off."

"Nothing to do with me? Like learning my father wasn't my father had nothing to do with you?" he asked, impressed when his voice sounded so deadly calm. Steely and sure.

Like Dad.

"Stop poking at this. Stop... Just stop."

He considered it, because he didn't want to sound or feel like Gerald. He didn't want her to be upset, especially when she was carrying their baby. He also didn't want to back down.

But there had to be a way to find some gentleness to exist even in all this anger.

He inhaled and exhaled and forced himself to unclench his hands. Forced himself to focus on *her*, not what he was feeling. He needed to let some of his own emotions go so he had room to absorb hers.

She was breathing rapidly, and her eyes kept darting anywhere but to him. She wasn't angry, or not only angry. She was *scared*. And he didn't think it was of him exactly. It was this talking that got her so panicked. He didn't understand it, and in the past he might have hinted around that. Or he might have ignored it.

Clearly, he'd made a mistake there. No more. "What are you so afraid of? Why can't we talk about this?"

She just looked at him, her mouth opening and then closing.

"Sierra. Just tell me. Tell me. We have to let this go. No matter what happens, divorce or not, we have to let some of this go."

"I wanted a baby!" she yelled at him, more tears falling from her eyes and just about doing him in. "I didn't want to go get a job or wait or anything. I just wanted to have a baby with you." She yelled it all, though it cracked at the end.

That hurt. Really hurt because a part of him had wondered, but when she'd agreed with him that she should find something for herself first, he'd let that wonder go. He'd been certain she'd agreed because she wanted to agree.

"Honey, why didn't you tell me?" His own voice cracked on the question even though she had sort of gotten what she wanted—they were going to have a baby in a few months. Still, that she'd kept that to herself, agreed with him when she hadn't wanted to... He reached out but she slapped his hand away and maneuvered off the wall.

"Tell you? So you could explain to me that I was wrong? So you could tell me all the rational, *good* reasons we should wait?"

"Well, that's a discussion, isn't it? I assume if you agree that you *agree*, not that you're just pawning me off so you don't have to have a discussion."

"It wouldn't have been a discussion!"

"Sierra—"

"You're the smart one. The *employed* one. You're always right. You make the decisions. That's our life. I wasn't about to ruin the status quo."

Except, this went back to the running-away thing. Because sometimes she did fight him, tell him he was wrong or that just because he was the 'smart' one didn't mean he got to decide everything.

But she lied and she ran away when things mattered. It was a step to realize it, to identify it.

But he had no idea where to go from here.

Chapter Ten

WHY WAS THIS happening? Why had she *said* any of that? She should have ignored him. She'd yelled at *him*. Horrible things she'd wanted to keep to herself forever. Like him wanting to wait to have a baby had planted an awful fear inside of her, and how everything about the following months had made it grow.

She'd never wanted him to know all that, but he wouldn't back off or down and now she was crying in front of him and it changed *nothing*.

Nothing.

"Can't you just leave me alone?" Alone to cry and hurt and give in to all this without him *seeing* it.

"It seems as though we've done a little bit too much of that."

It somehow hurt more because it was true. There had been too much alone and too many silences, but it was too late. You didn't fix silences because you couldn't go back and talk instead. They existed forever. They were a symptom of something else.

She tried to calm her shaky breath, the tears overflowing.

She had to be strong somehow. Because if she gave in to more of this she wouldn't just have a failed marriage, she'd have to remember this horrible, horrible moment for the rest of her life.

"If you won't leave, I'll leave," she managed to say, though she didn't think it sounded as strong out loud as she'd hoped it would. But it didn't matter. She moved for the door, certain, *certain,* Carter wouldn't follow.

But he moved in front of her, and he didn't stop with getting in her way. He took her by the shoulders, his big hands enveloping them, holding her tight and in place.

She wanted to push him and yell at him and tell him to let her go. She wanted to run away. But all she could seem to do was sob out a breath.

His hands came to her face, holding her there between them. Hands that had healed people and helped people and she'd never understood why he held her with such gentleness when there was so much inside of him and so little for her to offer.

There'd been blind faith once, but now it was gone. Still she couldn't seem to do anything but stand here and cry. Stand here and let him touch her as though she were something precious to him.

"Why do you always run away when it matters?" he asked, and his voice was low and rusty. *Emotional.* And confronting. She didn't want him to be hurt. Didn't want him…wanting things from her. Emotions and truths.

The silences had been better than this. Than ripping herself apart for the sake of nothing. The having him ask her in that *hurt* voice why she was running.

"Sierra. This matters. To you. To me. It's going to end up mattering to our child no matter what happens. I know it's hard and it hurts..." He gripped her face more firmly, tipping it so she looked up at him.

She closed her eyes against seeing all that hurt in the depths of his blue eyes.

"Cole gave me advice and I thought it was wrong and stupid, but maybe he really was right and I was wrong. Wouldn't that be funny?"

"Car—"

"Love is showing each other your cracks. Maybe more than that, maybe it's trusting each other with your flaws. Your imperfections. Neither of us have done that at all."

"I can't. I can't trust you with that," she managed to whisper. Even though the words were welling up inside of her. All those flaws. The things she'd ignored but here they were.

She opened her eyes when he said nothing, and it was worse than the determination and hurt that had been there when she'd closed them. His confusion was evident along with that hurt, and then a spark of desperation in the way he held her face, in the way his eyes were a little wild.

It was that more than anything that had the words tumbling out of her mouth. Broken up by sobs, but said nonetheless. He wanted her flaws? He wanted to make this harder than what it was? What choice did she have? He was the one who knew best. The one who made the choices.

"Just let me go, Carter. I'm not good enough for you."

"Sierra—"

"No. No, don't argue with me. You finally saw it—I know you did. Because you didn't turn to me when you were in your darkest hour. You shut me out because you knew I wasn't good enough to be at your side. And you were right. Completely, utterly right and I won't go back to wondering when the other shoe's going to drop. I'm not good enough. I was stupid to think I could pretend. So, let me go."

He exhaled, something close to a gasp as if she'd physically harmed him, and then his hands weren't on her face, they were around her, pulling her close and against him. He held her there, so tight she could barely breathe enough to cry, but the tears poured out of her anyway. The pain searing and deep.

But he pressed his forehead into the crook of her neck, holding her, whispering against her skin. "No. God. No."

She wanted to argue with him. *Yes! Let me go! Now!* But all she could do was cry into his hair. She shouldn't let him hold her, but it felt…

She'd been holding herself so tight, so apart. Even that night they'd made this child growing in her there'd been a silence, an edge keeping them apart. But this…

Against her will, against all her determinations, her muscles relaxed. She melted into him, truly and really. She cried all of her broken-hearted dreams out and into him, and he held her. Whispering words of love. Promises she couldn't ever believe again.

She didn't know how long it lasted, how many tears she had. But he held her through it all. He murmured everything she'd wanted to hear months ago, but even with all the crying she was numb to it.

"I love you," and it was said in that same vehement voice he'd used when she'd laughed the first time he'd said it to her. She'd laughed because she'd wanted so badly to tell him she loved him too. Because she knew she shouldn't. And he shouldn't.

She'd always known, but he'd used that voice and she'd been a goner. Look at where it had gotten her.

She had to find her strength. She had to walk away, but he punctuated those weaponized words with the brush of his mouth against her shoulder where her collar had slid down. He held her and he kissed her there.

"You're beautiful and bright. You make my dull, plodding life sparkle." He kissed her again, the brush of his lips up the curve of her neck would never, ever fail to make her knees go weak.

But she had to be strong. Tell him to stop. Words didn't change what they were, and what they couldn't be. Neither did the warm, lazy sensations spilling through her.

"You don't want your life to sparkle, Carter. You want it

to matter."

He paused briefly before his mouth brushed her cheek, featherlight, sweet. "I want both. I want you. I want to fight for this." His mouth closed over hers, insistent, needy. Vulnerable.

Carter McArthur vulnerable. She really had ruined him. Spread her brokenness or something and she couldn't stand it. She couldn't stand it. She had to do something to prove to him this was a mistake.

So, she kissed him back, because they'd done this a few weeks ago, hadn't they? Come together and he'd disappeared. Maybe they hadn't talked then like they'd talked now, but it was all the same.

A weakness. A lapse in judgment.

When she was gone when he woke up in the morning, he'd know, really know, how right she was.

And it'd all be over.

THERE WAS A strange moment in the kiss when Carter didn't think Sierra would reciprocate. He'd kissed her and for seconds she'd stood there like a statue, as if figuring out a difficult math equation while he poured his heart and soul into her.

But then her mouth moved under his. Not soft—and if it had been anything like the last time they'd done this he would have found that amazing. New. Hot.

But he was raw. *Raw*. Cut open and bleeding and he needed some softness. Some healing. So he swept his fingers into her hair, cupping her scalp, angling her head so he could settle himself at the corner of her mouth and make his way to the other side.

She let out a shuddery sigh, and though there was some acquiescence in that, there was also a band of tension in her. Even in kissing him, in crying into him, in holding each other, there were pieces of herself she was holding apart. Saving to give herself the fuel to run away.

He couldn't let that happen. He couldn't give her that, because while he was an expert in thinking he knew what was best for people, and probably being wrong on occasion, this wasn't like that. It wasn't in knowing better than her. It wasn't in having a better view on the situation.

It was seeing her fear, her insecurity, her *cracks* and needing to fill them. With love. With all the certainty he felt. Because she was wrong. She thought his silences had been about her, about her lack of worth.

Guilt, dark and vicious and ugly swept through him, but he didn't let that leak into his kiss, into the gentle way he held her hair.

He'd been worse than an idiot, worse than blind, but the only way to fix that, to make up for it, to learn and heal and grow from that horrible mistake was to show her the opposite of what he'd shown her then.

No silences, no keeping himself apart because he'd felt less and worthless from the knowledge of his parentage. No withdrawing until he connected all the dots by himself.

Marriage and love weren't about only giving the best to each other, something he still had trouble really wrapping his head around. But the truth of it existed in her tears, in this *pain*. Making a relationship work was about turning to each other, even when it was hard, even when it didn't make sense, even when the thing you most wanted to do in the world was turn away and protect your already bruised heart.

"I've made such a mess of things," he murmured against her mouth, and then her temple. "We've made such a mess of things," he corrected, because silences went two ways. They'd each been silent for similar reasons, both been too afraid to reach out for the other.

"Yes," she agreed, tilting her head so his mouth could trail down her neck. "It's not the kind of mess you can clean up."

He stopped, though he kept his hands in her hair as he pulled his head away to look down at her. Misery, exhaustion, and yet she didn't push him away. She didn't tell him to stop.

He dropped his forehead to hers, looking into her wary eyes. He couldn't cure her wariness. Couldn't convince her it was a mess they *would* clean up. Not in all the ways he was used to or understood. Reason and talking wouldn't solve this problem.

He vowed to solve it anyway. To talk through it. To keep showing up. To ask Cole for a million pieces of advice. To never turn away from Sierra again no matter how much he wanted to keep his hurt to himself where it felt like it belonged.

But a vow he made to himself didn't count, did it? Wasn't that the point of all this? It didn't matter if she believed him, if she thought he was weak or wrong. The vow, his intention—telling it to her was the thing that mattered.

"I don't believe that. We can fix this," he said roughly, holding her tight when she tried to look away. "I love you. I *want* you. The whole of who you are, the whole of what I love, is not the mistakes we made, Sierra."

"I need you to let me go."

He knew she didn't just mean physically. Because she could certainly pull his hands off her face. She could move out of his grasp.

But she didn't. She didn't.

"I'm not ever letting you go," he said. "You need me to hold on."

"Don't tell me what I ne—"

He covered her mouth with his, pouring everything he was into that kiss. Everything she meant. Words were important, and so were actions. The whole of it was important, not just one thing or the other. Not just being perfect or being imperfect.

It was the *all* of himself that he needed to give her, and maybe if he could do that, she'd trust him enough to give it back. Even if she didn't now, he'd keep doing it until she could.

"We did it all wrong there for a while," he said, punctuating the words with kisses as he moved her back toward the bed. "But we can fix that. We can *change* that. I believe that."

"I don't," she whispered, but her eyes were wide and open instead of hard. When he laid her out on the bed, she went easily, stretching out on the soft blankets and big mattress. "I don't believe it at all."

Now, he told himself. *She doesn't believe it now, but you can change that.* He had to change it. "Let me," he murmured.

"Let you what?" she asked, new tears forming in her eyes. But she lay there, and he had to believe this was a start. An opening.

This was what Cole had talked about when he'd said hard work and trying hard weren't the same. Trying hard meant hurting and failing and going on anyway. It meant things took time even when you didn't want them to.

It meant giving yourself even when you weren't guaranteed anything back.

He slowly lifted the hem of her sweatshirt up. She didn't stop him. In fact, she moved so he could lift it off of her completely, and then she lay back down. He tugged down the stretchy pants she wore, until she was lying underneath him in nothing but her underwear.

His gorgeous wife, pale skin and the colorful smattering of tattoos on one arm. Freckles on her shoulder and nose like gold dust. She looked impossibly vulnerable when he'd always seen her as a force of nature.

She was both, of course, and it was a revelation to realize she, and he, could be both. Weak and strong. Right and wrong. Insecure and sure.

"Let me show you."

Chapter Eleven

SIERRA WAS ALL mixed up. She'd decided to let him, to have this again just this once—she was *pregnant* after all. Then she'd leave. She would. She had to.

But who was this man kissing down her body like she was something not just precious or important but actually *necessary*, elemental to his survival?

Who was the man with these words? These promises? What had gone so warped in his head that he thought he should give them to *her*?

Still he hooked his fingers in the band of her panties and slowly slid them off her, and she didn't stop him. Didn't want to. As much as those words had reached inside of her and clawed at what little strength she had left, his touch was a balm. His gentle kiss against her knee, her thigh was warmth and *pleasure*.

She hadn't felt good since the last time they'd done this. That had been fleeting too, but it had been a hope dashed. This wouldn't be hope. It would just be goodbye.

Then his mouth was *on* her and there was no thought, no goodbye considerations, just sensation and pleasure as he licked into her. She let it sweep over her, hot and greedy. She opened for him, gasped for him, reveled in something so simple.

Love was supposed to be this simple. Not hard and fighting and mistakes. It was supposed to sweep over you like pleasure. Make your skin warm and your body hum. What was the point if it didn't work just like this?

But that was thinking and she didn't want to think. She wanted to *feel*. Carter's mouth against the most intimate part of her, the rising tension of pleasure, and then that glorious break and uncoiling of perfect, untethered bliss.

She let out a dreamy sigh as he moved off of her. He pulled off his shirt, his eyes on hers, blue and blazing. She simply watched as he undressed himself the rest of the way.

Tears and sadness threatened because he was so beautiful and he'd been hers for such a short period of time. She thought she'd have forever to memorize the muscles of his shoulders, that square jaw and the way it clenched when he was desperate for her.

She thought she'd watch this man grow old and—

And she couldn't think about it. She simply couldn't. So she moved into a sitting position and took off her bra so she was completely naked for him like he was for her. He crawled over her as she lay back down, intense and so determined.

She held her breath, waiting for that moment when he'd enter her, when he'd make the whole world fall away and this horrible clutching pain in her chest would disappear.

His eyes were so blue and they took up the whole world. How she wanted him to be her world. If only she were enough.

"I love you, Sierra," he murmured, sliding into her in a smooth, gentle stroke.

If only they could exist here. Perfectly joined. Her brain emptied and quiet as sensation took over.

Moving together, holding on to each other, breath and souls mingling. Where the outside world and real life didn't matter.

It should be this easy, shouldn't it? Wasn't that the point? Things that were simple and easy and only brought joy.

But even as they moved together she knew that didn't make any sense. Oh, she wanted it to, desperately, but his words from earlier were stronger and better somehow.

No. No. That was her insecurity talking and she had to be strong enough to protect herself. She had to be a good mother to this child inside of her and that meant not letting someone else guide her life or make her miserable.

"Sierra," Carter murmured into her neck, sliding his hand down her hip, holding her there as he moved. "I love you."

And he kept saying it, against her neck, against her lips, moving with her as she tried to shut it all out and focus on the building sensations inside of her instead of her heart swelling too big, too soft.

"Sierra."

She met his gaze, so serious, so *determined*, and while he'd always been a goal-oriented man, a man who worked hard and went after what he wanted, she'd never seen this ferocity, this *fire*.

"Say it back," he said, on a growl. "Mean it."

She blinked, trying to keep the tears at bay, trying to find this horrible instead of wonderful. Trying to ignore the way pleasure spread through her at that intensity, that demand. All the while moving, holding her and ratcheting her closer to that beautiful edge all over again.

"Sierra."

She wanted to fight him, but how did you fight the ocean? Blue and ceaseless. Big and vast and swallowing her whole.

"I love you, Carter," she said on a choked whisper, the orgasm ripping through her in a hot, tight rush, his following on a moan.

They lay there, her under the heavy, warm weight of him, holding on to each other as if they'd drift away without that link.

She must have fallen asleep, because when she woke up—tangled up in Carter, warm and happy and both of them still naked—a very dim light crept through the slight gap in the curtains he'd drawn afterward. It was just barely dawn, if she had to guess.

She moved her head and simply stared at Carter. He'd said so many things last night, *done* so many things. She couldn't wrap her head around why he didn't seem different. Still handsome as an angel, still her strong, awe-inspiring husband.

Even after admitting his mistakes and telling her he'd been wrong. Even calling the past few months a mess. Admitting his mistakes and pointing out hers and it didn't feel as though it had diminished either of them.

He'd asked her why she ran away when things got hard, and in the moment she hadn't known, but right here, she knew without a doubt.

Failure was so much more bearable when you could say you hadn't tried all that hard.

Was she going to try now?

She looked at his golden lashes against his cheeks, the way his hair had a little curl to it since it was getting too long. The golden glint of a five-o'clock shadow and the peaceful smile of a man who'd had thoroughly enjoyable sex last night.

If she tried now and still lost, how would she ever endure it? If she fell deeper, harder, entwined her life with his even tighter…

She couldn't do it. She had to be a mother to her child, and she'd never be able to if she started that journey with Carter as a partner.

Panic beat through her, not just in her chest but also in

her neck, in her head, in her wrists. Everywhere she throbbed with panic, struggling to breathe as she detangled herself from Carter.

He didn't budge, instead kept sleeping happily on.

She grabbed her clothes with shaky hands and managed to get them back on her body before slipping out the bedroom door.

She padded into the kitchen, feeling like a criminal. Her heart beat too hard and she jumped at every noise. She was shaking, couldn't breathe right, and every cell in her being was telling her to go back to bed and *believe*.

But her brain reminded her of all the reasons why she shouldn't. It might not have control over her body's reactions to leaving, but it knew what was right.

She shoved her feet into her shoes and shrugged on her coat. She closed her hand over Carter's keys and paused, looking at the sparkling rings on her finger.

This had to be it. Much more and he'd win and she'd...

What? Be happy and whole?

She shook away that traitorous thought. Because the truth didn't exist in *hope*, the truth existed in experience. Her experience was she and Carter couldn't do this.

Or maybe it was just her. *She* couldn't do it. She would never belong in a place like this. She would never survive years of cleaning up messes and making things work. She wasn't strong enough.

So, she snuck out the front door, got in his car, and

started driving.

※

CARTER ROLLED OVER in bed, perfectly warm and satisfied for the first time in months. *Months.* Sierra wasn't in bed. But he heard someone out in the kitchen so he didn't have to panic.

He felt whole again, all those fractures after Dad had dropped his bomb healed.

Objectively, he knew they probably weren't *healed* precisely. But he'd had all his priorities skewed. Thinking everything in life was McArthurs and putting forth a good image and being a respected doctor.

But he should have been worried about being a husband and a partner. It should be more important to be a *good* doctor rather than a respected one. Once upon a time those had been his tenets, but he'd morphed into his father's way of thinking about things. They weren't necessarily wrong ways of thinking, but they were too rigid and harsh. It didn't leave room for *him.*

So he'd put in the hard work, he'd try, over and over again until it all worked. Which was life, really. As a doctor, if he stepped back and looked at the whole of life, the body was a thing of balance. You never knew when things would throw it out of whack, when things would threaten survival, when time and toil changed the way a body did things.

Life was just like that. Never perfect, though sometimes good enough you barely noticed the time passing. But problems always cropped up, and ignoring those issues rarely made them better.

He should tell that analogy to Sierra. She might not appreciate it as much as his doctor brain did, but maybe it'd clarify where he was coming from.

On a yawn he rolled out of bed and pulled on his boxers and headed for the kitchen to see what she was up to. Except there was no lively blonde in the cabin's kitchen.

"Lina." His sister's presence made...zero sense.

She turned from where she'd been looking out one of the kitchen windows that offered a view of the slew of evergreens dashed with snow. She wrinkled her nose. "Ew, put some clothes on."

But that didn't penetrate at all. "What are you doing here? Where's Sierra?"

Her face changed, going soft, which was not a Lina trait at all. She looked away. "Go get dressed, Carter."

But he simply stood there absorbing...this. Lina was here. Sierra was not.

His sister was here.

His wife was not.

It reminded Carter of the moment after his father had announced he wasn't actually Carter's father. There was a kind of numbness that spread from that deep flash of pain. Denial and impossible disappointment twined together to make the entire world feel frozen.

But he forced his feet to move, retrace his steps, go into the bedroom to find his clothes. He stopped in the doorway, looking at the rumpled bed, and he didn't...

She'd left. After all they'd shared, after all he'd laid bare. She still *left*. Without the courtesy of an explanation or a goodbye.

As though he didn't matter, as though nothing they'd ever had mattered. He walked over to the bed with the intention of grabbing his jeans where they lay in a heap on the floor.

Instead he found himself sinking onto the mattress, lowering his head to his hands. He'd tried, put his all, his heart and soul into repairing things. Into her. And he still hadn't gotten the result he'd wanted.

She'd left. It was all a failure. A new kind of failure because any time he'd considered failure in the past it wasn't like this. It was worrying his father would find out and be disappointed. It was worrying about reputation and what others thought, not the actual failure result.

This... He couldn't bring himself to worry about his family's opinion or what the town or hospital would whisper behind his back. All he cared about was the fact Sierra wasn't *here*, after all the inroads he'd thought he'd made and she'd still run away.

He lifted his head, frowning. She ran away from things that mattered. He thought he'd gotten through to her, but apparently he hadn't. At least not enough. He could give up, let that feel like a failure. Or...

She ran away when things *mattered*. Who was he to think one night would fix that pattern? Giving up now would only put them back to where they'd been, and he wouldn't go back there. No amount of failures could allow him to forget he had to keep trying, because as long as she was running, this was something worth fighting for.

Yes. No matter how many failures or setbacks. He pulled on his pants and shirt and then went back to the kitchen where Lina was sitting at the table, sipping tea.

"So, what exactly are you doing here?" he demanded.

She frowned, presumably at the tone, but she shifted uncomfortably, her eyes darting anywhere but to him. "Well, Sierra asked me to come get you since she, you know, took your car."

"Right. Did she say anything else?"

"Uh." Lina winced. "No. Just to get you home."

"Of course." It might hurt, but he would take it as a good sign. He wasn't sure what had happened in his life to make hurt a good sign, but she'd disappeared early in the morning. She'd left no note, no words not to follow. It meant she'd been driven by panic, not rational thinking.

He had to believe that.

"You're kind of freaking me out," Lina said, studying him uncertainly.

"Why?"

"You're calm, but kind of like...murdery underneath that."

"I'm not murdery," he replied darkly, moving for his shoes and coat. "I'm determined."

"Determined to commit murder?"

"No. Now, stop sitting around chatting and relaxing—I have things to do."

"What kind of things?"

"Find my wife things. What else would there be?"

"She sounded... Maybe you should give her some space. She was upset when she called me. Afraid, almost. I'm not saying she's afraid of *you*, just... She's struggling. You should give her space."

"Why?" Carter demanded, shrugging on his coat once his shoes were tied.

"What do you mean, why?"

"Why should I give her space when she's upset and struggling?"

"Because people want to be alone when they feel like crap," Lina said stubbornly, her scowl awfully deep for someone who, as far as he knew, had never even dated.

"No. I mean, maybe sometimes. We're talking about people, and people are different and complex and flawed. There's no one solution fits all, but Sierra... Look, she needs—"

Lina snorted. "I'm sorry, I find it really hard to believe you know what she needs."

He looked at his sister then, really looked. In some ways, they were nothing alike. Lina had a sharp tongue and the older she got the less afraid she was to use it. But she could be hard and judgmental, and in that way he saw himself.

It softened him in some ways, because he knew that the hardness stemmed from trying to protect themselves. A shell they'd all grown in the face of their parents' demanding expectations.

"Maybe I don't know what she needs, but I know she's scared. I know she's running because she's afraid that I can't be what she needs. Why would I let her keep thinking that? Even if it's not what she needs, though I have my doubts on that, I'll never give someone I love the space to think the worst again. Not after dealing with the aftermath of that. I have to keep showing up even if it's just to stand there."

Lina frowned deeper, but she didn't continue her argument.

"So, where is she?"

"I don't know. She just told me she took your car and you needed a ride home."

"Then I don't need a ride home. I need a ride to her."

Lina's expression went a little soft. "Carter..."

"Help me find her, Lina. Please."

"I think that's the first time you've ever said *please* to me and actually meant it."

"Well, that's going to change." A lot of things were.

Chapter Twelve

SIERRA HAD SPENT the morning driving around in Carter's car. She should have returned it. She should have gone home, but she wasn't ready to face anyone. So, she'd driven to the closest town from the McArthur cabin and gotten breakfast to go. She'd even filled up his gas tank as she'd driven in a meandering, back-roads fashion back to Marietta.

It had felt nice, kind of. Nothing but silence and gorgeous mountains and a pretty Montana morning. She'd never loved being alone, but there was something in it that gave her room to work through her thoughts, her feelings, her panic.

She'd hoped for the kind of clarifying moment she'd had in that Walmart bathroom. Was that only a week or so ago? It felt like years. Years and years ago.

But it hadn't been, and instead of that absolutely sure resolution she'd made in that bathroom, she drove into Marietta feeling as unsure and confused as ever.

She didn't want to leave Carter. She hadn't wanted to leave that cabin. Love and being with him were *good* and she wanted those things. She wanted to believe everything he said about cracks and love and the things you had to do.

But no matter how much those things resonated, no matter how much she wondered if fixing this wasn't the right answer, fear lingered.

Would this much fear linger if love was enough? She didn't doubt they loved each other, what she doubted was the ability of love to survive...*life*. Or maybe even her.

She couldn't face her parents with all this uncertainty. Not when they knew she'd been gone overnight and Carter had been the one to contact them and tell her where she was. They'd be expecting things and she wouldn't know how to answer.

Not without showing them all her cracks. And there was all that fear again, mixed in with this new...desire. Almost as if she kind of wanted to let them see all her insecurities so they understood for once why she was the way she was.

Damn Carter. He'd messed her all up. She needed someone who'd talk some sense into her. Someone who saw her for what she was. Who knew how awful she could be and would support her in the very real knowledge that she, *she*, could not do this. She wasn't strong enough for love and cracks and years upon years. Yes, that's exactly what she needed.

She drove to Kaitlin's apartment above the florist shop. It wasn't fair to bother Kaitlin when she had a *newborn*, but Sierra was too mixed up to worry about fair. Too desperate for someone to reassure her what she knew to be true...was.

She parked and then went to the back and up the stairs to Kaitlin and Beckett's apartment.

She knocked and Kaitlin answered, baby Ellie all curled up into her chest.

Sierra's own chest clutched tight. She was going to have one of those. A tiny, defenseless human being, and she was going to have to be strong enough to protect her or him, raise them to be good, upstanding people.

She rubbed at her chest as her sister's expression registered surprise.

"Sierra."

"Sorry. I know you're probably like a million times exhausted and I didn't tell you I was coming."

"I'm glad you're here," Kaitlin said, moving aside so Sierra could step in. Kaitlin's normally tidy place was a haphazard mess of baby things. "Beckett had to go into work for a few hours and it's just me and Ellie and I know I shouldn't be, but I'm terrified. I have to pee, but she cries every time I put her down and—"

Sierra held out her arms. "Give her to me. Pee."

"God *bless* you," Kaitlin said vehemently, handing Ellie over carefully and then rushing to the bathroom.

Sierra stood in the midst of a messy whirlwind, this tiny, *tiny* little thing in her arms. Ellie blinked up at Sierra, her dark blue eyes seeming to take in Sierra's face. Then she made a snorting noise, closed her eyes, and settled against

Sierra's arm.

When Kaitlin reappeared, Sierra surveyed her older sister. Kaitlin's hair looked a bit like a rat's nest, she had bags under her eyes, and there were spots here and there on the shoulders of her shirt.

"You could have called Mom. Or me," Sierra said gently.

"I know, but I need to learn how to do it on my own. I *wanted* to do it on my own. I just… She's so little."

"It's a miracle how tiny."

Kaitlin collapsed onto the couch so Sierra sat down on the opposite end, enjoying the feeling of tiny, warm dozing baby in her arms. It was almost enough to make her problems feel far away.

But she'd come here *about* her problems, hadn't she? She couldn't exactly ignore them forever. Lina had probably already made it out to the cabin to pick up Carter and he'd likely be wanting his car back.

But Kaitlin was slumped on the couch, eyes half closed.

"You look like you could use a nap."

"I could use a coma," Kaitlin replied, but she smiled as she said it. "Or maybe just a bigger house. Beckett's been taking the night wake-ups, but I can't sleep through it anyway."

"How's he handling the daddy business?"

Kaitlin's smile bloomed even more. "It really is something to watch the man you love be a dad." At that, Kaitlin straightened a bit and glanced Sierra's way. "So."

"So." Sierra let out a long sigh. "So." She should open with something that made sense. A segue of sorts. Instead... "I slept with Carter. Again."

Kaitlin's eyes went wide. "So, you're going to work things out?"

Sierra looked down at the baby's closed eyes and slightly open mouth. "No, I... No."

"It might be the baby brain, but I'm confused."

"I'm not cut out for this whole...thing."

"Marriage?"

"Yes. Marriage. Love. You have to... You know me, Kaitlin. You grew up with me. I'm not cut out for hard stuff. I don't have your strength or Luke's grit. I'm not smart. I don't have any interests. I'm just... I'm not cut out to be the wife of someone like Carter."

Kaitlin studied her for a few seconds and Sierra frowned because she did not see what she expected to, which was pure agreement. Or even reluctant agreement.

"I don't believe in *cut out*, Sierra," Kaitlin said, and it wasn't in that careful about-to-let-you-down-easy way. It was fierce. It reminded her of the way Carter had talked to her yesterday. "I believe in the choices we make. They aren't always easy or fun, but they're ours, and they determine our future."

"I'm choosing to save him from—"

"Does he want to be saved from you?"

Sierra wanted to pace, but Ellie was so content in her

arms, so she had to stay still under Kaitlin's steady gaze.

"You don't understand. You always do the right thing. You always have. I have always done the wrong thing, and I always will. Carter and I will always circle back to these awful moments where it doesn't work. I can't stand the thought. I can't survive it."

"Did you expect to get married and everything would just be perfect? You'd always get along and be happy because you loved each other?"

"Yes! That's how love is supposed to work. It's supposed to be happy and easy or why would people do it?" Why would *love* be the thing that made the world go round if it could hurt this much? If it meant failure over and over again?

Kaitlin blew out a breath and rubbed her hand over her forehead. "Sierra, I'm no expert, but speaking from my experience and my experience alone… Look, I'm not speaking bad against Mom and Dad when I say this, because I know they always did what they thought was best. They were and are amazing parents. But I think… Marrying Beckett and having this beautiful girl I sort of realized our parents taught us that if we did everything right, everything would work out. But life doesn't work like that. It's imperfect and messy and right doesn't always make sense, which means just like sometimes the person who does everything right doesn't get everything she wants—the person who does everything wrong *does*."

Sierra didn't want it to hurt, but it did, because Kaitlin

was clearly the *did everything right* and she was so completely the *did everything wrong*. But Kaitlin reached over, squeezing her shoulder reassuringly.

"I'd like to point out, I *never* did everything right, and you *never* did everything wrong. We're human. We're complicated. Life isn't that cut and dried, and neither are we. It's funny, Beckett wasn't supposed to be right, but he's the best thing that's ever happened to me. Even when we fight. Even when it hurts. It's not love if it doesn't hurt a little. Loving someone is always going to hurt a little, if only because you're both human. You'll hurt each other. It's in the making up you find yourselves."

"It hurts more than a little." It hurt like it'd never heal. Like she'd always be this cracked apart and alone.

"Love is in the hurts—as much as it's in the way you come away from the hurts. Life is hard. It throws a lot at you, and love is just another way to lose. That's true. But it's also the only way to win. Love does make you better. I think, even if you don't realize it or feel it, loving someone makes you a better person."

"What if it doesn't?" She didn't feel like a better person. She felt as mixed up as she'd always been, with a heaping dose of *you don't deserve him* on the side.

"Sierra, I don't know what's happened between you and Carter. I do know… We didn't used to talk. You used to not be able to be in a room with Mom and Dad without completely losing it if they dare suggest you do anything. I'm not saying because of Carter that happened, but maybe loving Carter helped you love us a little more, open up to us a little more. I think sometimes when you learn to love one person, it can't help but spread. I know that's what happened for me."

It was...true. Weirdly. Inside she felt like she hadn't changed at all, but Kaitlin was right. All they used to do was fight or say snide things to each other, and that hadn't been all Sierra. Kaitlin had been judgmental and mean all on her own, but she'd mellowed in the past year. Love had changed her.

Then there was her parents. All Sierra had done with them for years was snipe, try to protect herself by lashing out.

She hadn't felt compelled to engage in either behavior with her family in quite a while. Had she really changed? Grown? It made sense, and she wanted to blame the kind of maturity that came with age, but it was hard to deny that learning to handle how much she loved Carter had taught her some things about love and people in general.

"The thing is, and again, I speak from my own narrow experience here: the problem is not in being strong enough or good enough or right enough to love Carter. You love him anyway, or you wouldn't be this miserable. The problem is you have to figure out how to love yourself, because it's really hard to build a relationship, a partnership—marriage and parenting—when you're busy thinking they shouldn't be giving you all you're giving them. It's awfully hard to build a partnership on unequal footing."

"How could I ever be on equal footing with him? He's smart and driven and—"

"And didn't he not talk to you for practically *months* because he couldn't deal with his family stuff? Sorry, Sierra, he might be a great guy, but he isn't perfect."

Lina had basically said the same thing. And it was particularly weird because up until these past few weeks she'd never heard anyone talk bad about Carter. He and Cole hadn't gotten along, but she'd figured it was in the same way she and Kaitlin hadn't. Good and bad. Right and wrong.

Not that this was talking *bad* exactly, but Kaitlin was being critical of Carter, the way Lina had been, the way her parents had been, when before this breakup people were usually only critical of Sierra.

But that was awfully simple, wasn't it? She'd expected adulthood and love to be simple, but... What would ever be simple about two separate people joining lives? What would ever be simple about dealing with parents' illnesses and time demands from jobs or what have you? If she really thought about what the future held, there would be *nothing* simple about raising a child. Even for Carter.

"Think about it this way, Sierra. I love you. Carter loves you. Mom and Dad love you. Luke loves you. You're close with Carter's sister too, right? And Jess Clark. I'd be willing to bet they love you too. Are we all so wrong?"

"You might be," Sierra muttered.

"We're not. You're funny and I always admired how you followed the beat of your own drum. I was jealous of it. You aren't perfect, but neither am I, and most definitely neither is Carter. It's a process, and it's not all at once nor does it need to be, but you need to learn to love yourself. Because he loves you, and you love him. Which means you're both worth that hard work to make your relationship work. Maybe you have to make some changes, and you definitely have to work together to communicate what you need, but if he loves you, Sierra, if he's fighting for you, wanting to make it work, that's the only thing you need to know."

"I don't want to be torn apart again. Have him turn away from me because..." Carter had admitted he'd been wrong, but that didn't mean he wouldn't do it again. Of course, he wasn't in the habit of saying things he didn't mean. But still, there were things that would happen that would hurt and... "I can't do it. I can't watch him look at me and know he thinks I'm less, even if I am."

"Sierra. He doesn't think you're less. He married you, and he clearly doesn't want to divorce you. *You* think you're less, and that's something you're going to have to deal with. Because he can't make you think you're more. You have to decide you are."

She'd come here for Kaitlin to confirm her concerns, not... Not turn it around so she was responsible for doing some changing.

"And even beyond being enough or less or not…" Kaitlin reached out and touched Sierra's stomach. "I hate to break it to you, and I know I'm still new to this motherhood thing, but Mom warned me. Your kids are going to hurt you. Over and over again. When they don't know any better, and then when they do, too. Because they're their own people. They get to make their own choices and you can't control them, or make them what you want them to be. You love them with everything you are, want to save them and protect them and give them everything. And it's never going to work."

"Great pep talk, Mom," Sierra muttered.

Kaitlin laughed. "God, it sounds awful, doesn't it? I think her point was to not put stress on myself to do all the right things. Because motherhood, and life, don't work that way. What I'm trying to impart to you, not so well, is that you can't insulate yourself from hurt. You're going to be a mother. Things are going to be hard and they're going to hurt. That doesn't mean you're wrong or it's not worth it. Because the thing that makes it worth it all is love, and this I know even after a few days. The love you feel for that little baby you're growing in there will knock you flat."

Sierra would have put her hand over her stomach, but she was holding Ellie with both arms. "How am I going to survive *that*?" Sierra whispered.

"The same way women always survive it. Working hard, loving fiercely, and asking for help when you need it."

"So, maybe calling someone when you have to pee and you're afraid to put the baby down?"

Kaitlin wrinkled her nose, but her mouth curved. "It's a work in progress. And that's life too."

A work in progress. Now that, *that* made a certain kind of sense. Maybe she didn't even have to feel like she was good enough for Carter, or comfortable with showing him her cracks, or *ready* to face everything she was going to have to face.

But maybe she could try. And keep trying. Progress, not perfection.

Because, much to her surprise, she did have a whole legion of people who loved her. Who supported her. If she'd opened up to any one of them before she'd been completely at rock bottom, what might have changed?

What might still change?

Chapter Thirteen

LINA HAD DRIVEN Carter back to Marietta. They'd gone up and down just about every street and side street. He'd had Lina drive by Sierra's parents' house, the florist shop where Kaitlin and Beckett lived, and even passed Sierra's brother's house. But Carter hadn't spotted his car anywhere.

"Where the hell could she be?" Carter muttered. "Has she texted you back?"

"No. She knows I'm with you though, or at least might assume since she called me to pick you up. We could stop by the hospital and try to catch Jess. Sierra might respond to Jess."

"Just…take me home."

Lina spared him a glance. "So, you're giving up?"

"No. I'm starving and I have a headache. I'm going to go home, eat something, take an aspirin, and then I'll call her parents. If they don't know where she is, well, then I get to worry."

"You shouldn't worry *them*. Wherever she is, she's fine and she'll let you know when she's ready—"

"Just take me home, Lina. I'll handle the rest."

She huffed out an irritated breath and rolled her eyes, scowling as she headed for his house.

He wasn't sure what compelled him when his sister was so completely Team Sierra and prickly at best and he'd never been her favorite person, but he didn't think that should be the last thing he said to her today.

"Thank you for your help. It means a lot."

She shrugged jerkily. "Whatever."

"No. Not whatever. You took time out of your day and life to come pick me up then drive me around, and I know it's because you care about Sierra. I appreciate that."

"I care about both of you, dumb ass," she grumbled, eyes firmly on the road ahead of her.

"I care about you too."

"Carter. Look."

He looked away from her to the view ahead of them. As they approached his house, he could see what Lina wanted him to look at.

His car. Parked in the drive. The car Sierra had taken this morning. Lina pulled up next to it and Carter simply sat there.

"Do you think she's here?" Lina asked incredulously. "After all that, she was here all along?"

"The lights are on," Carter noted. It wasn't dark yet, but the afternoon had turned the kind of gray that made it feel much later than it was. "I didn't leave the lights on."

"Well. Are you going to go in and find out or are you going to sit here?"

He felt rooted to the spot. Hope a terrible thing bubbling through him, because she might not be in there. Or she might be in there, just gathering up her things to leave again. There were so many ways she could crush his hope, and as much as he'd determined to keep trying, he needed to be ready to face possible disappointment. Tamp down this surging, desperate hope. "I shouldn't get my hopes up."

"Nope," Lina agreed, too readily for his tastes.

"She probably just got a bunch of her stuff and left," Carter decided, because if he said all the negative possibilities out loud he'd be ready for them. He could roll with the punches.

Funny all the ways actually communicating had the potential to help.

"Probably," Lina agreed again, but when he still just sat there she sighed. "Or, she's in there. So, why don't you go find out?"

"Right. Okay."

"It'll be okay either way. Because you're not giving up, right? So, even if it doesn't go well like this morning, you're going to…" She waved a hand between them. "Keep trying or whatever."

"Even when it's hard. Even when I fail," he said, more to himself than Lina.

"Then get the hell out of my car."

Yes. He needed to move. It took a while to get his head and his body on the same wavelength, but eventually he got out of the car. It felt like his body was weighted with lead. Even his heart beat faster and harder against all that.

He didn't have his house keys, he realized, because Sierra had taken his entire key ring to drive his car. So, if she wasn't here, he was kind of screwed.

On a deep breath, he raised his hand to knock. "Screw that," he muttered. It was his house as much as hers, and she'd walked out on him this morning. He could damn well walk into their home.

As long as it wasn't locked. He tested the knob and when it gave he felt some kind of relief. There was a bone-numbing fear there too, but he brazened through it, striding into the house.

He wasn't sure where he expected to find her. He had an image of her in their bedroom completely clearing out her side of the closet instead of just the missing chunk he'd been staring at for days. Another of her dumping all of her toiletries into a bag and sailing out of the house.

If he pictured them, he could survive them. Or so he told himself.

But instead of any bad scenarios, she stepped into the space between the living room and the kitchen, staring at him with an expression he couldn't read.

It reminded him of that night all those weeks ago. He'd come home simply to change, exhausted and numb. All he'd wanted to do was curl up in bed with her, but Mom had been demanding she needed him or she didn't know what she'd do.

Sierra had stood right there, staring at him with that same unreadable cast to her features. Then she'd followed him into the bedroom. He'd been weighed down by that numb feeling, but she followed and when she had, the pain leaked through.

It was why he'd stayed silent and distant for all that time. He couldn't be strong around her, couldn't keep it together. So, he'd had to keep her at arm's length, to keep the pain and confusion from pouring out and into her. But then she'd kissed him and...

A better man would have resisted, or so he'd thought at the time. Now, knowing it had given him the opportunity to be a father, a chance to come out of that horrible fog, well, maybe he'd been the best man he could be.

"Hi," she finally offered, still standing where she was, still expressionless.

"You're here."

She stood there looking... He didn't have any words aside from *perfect*. Wearing the same clothes she'd had on yesterday, her hair pulled back sloppily. She still had that paleness to her, a weariness. But she was *here*.

"I'm here," she said carefully. Too carefully.

He couldn't take it. What did he care if he was strong? What did it matter if she stomped all over his heart again?

He didn't have to be strong for her. He had to be honest. "I'm going to need you to tell me right here, right now, if you being here means something."

"I'm not sure it means everything," she said, her voice quiet and wavery. "But it means something."

That was all he needed to cross the distance, pull her into his arms, and kiss her with every last ounce of relief that coursed through him.

Without a hint of hesitation, she kissed him back. Soft and sweet and, hopefully not just his wishful thinking, filled with her own relief. All through last night he'd thought he was getting through to her, reaching her, but he'd known, ignored but known, she'd been holding pieces of herself back.

Because this, *this* was everything. Soft and relaxed, honest and pure. This was hope.

"Carter," she said, holding him off though *not* pushing him away. "We have to talk."

"I know. God, I know. Just once more." And he gave himself leave to kiss her until he shook, until she trembled, and until the entire world seemed so far away they both had to blink when they pulled away as if coming back to earth.

Her eyes glowed something like golden, wet with tears, but her mouth wasn't that horrible desolate frown from the past few days, months if he was honest with himself. And boy was it time to be honest with himself, and her.

"I am so sorry for shutting you out. I know I hurt you,

and I couldn't see past my own hurt to see it in you."

"And I didn't tell you I was hurting. Not...really. We retreated into our shells, and I blamed you and you..."

"Being around you hurt, because I wanted... You are life, *my* life, and I didn't want to have to figure out how to live a life where I wasn't his. But that was stupid. Because I'm yours, and you're mine."

Her mouth curved at that. "We should get that tattooed on our foreheads."

He grinned in response. "Sierra, for you, I'd get it tattooed anywhere."

But she looked down, some of that humor leaving her face. Still he held her, and he waited, because *that* was marriage, and he was learning to be a hell of a lot better at it.

SIERRA SWALLOWED AT the nerves coating her throat. Just because she'd decided what to do didn't make it easy.

She just had to say it. It couldn't be worse than losing him. It couldn't be. It *wouldn't* be. She could choose to make it what she wanted it to be. "I don't think I'm good enough for you."

"I think that's bullshit," he returned emphatically.

She raised her gaze to meet his. She liked this new fierceness to him, and she knew she'd find some of her own. Because *that* was love. She'd teach him fun. He'd teach her fierce. And so on, forever and ever, till death did they part.

Because she and he would choose to make this work. Here. Now. Doubts were for voicing, for talking through. Then they didn't have any power.

"But your family doesn't think it's bullshit, and I know they're your family, and I'm not saying you have to cut them off, but it's hard to believe in yourself when you're constantly dressed down by someone you know the person you love loves. If that makes sense."

He listened to her carefully, and she knew the difference because he didn't always. She was under no illusion that he'd start being perfect. She certainly tuned him out when he got going on about something medical she didn't understand, but maybe if they learned to recognize it in each other, ask for the attention to be paid...

It was daunting all the *work* that would need to be put into her marriage now. When she'd said 'I do' to Carter she thought it would be fun and easy. She thought love was a cure-all for life's problems.

Cure-alls didn't exist, but love did cushion the blows. It held you up and kissed you and made you laugh, and if she had to work to have those good things when the hard times inevitably rolled around again, and again, it'd be worth it.

She'd somehow come to believe in the course of these past twenty-four hours it would be worth it. Some mix of Carter's love, and Kaitlin pointing out Sierra already was a better version of herself, and then Beckett coming home and scooping up Ellie and kissing Kaitlin and looking at them both with such *awe*.

She wanted that.

"I'm not sure how to handle my family," Carter said, pained. "I wish I had a pill I could prescribe them to make them not be so hard. I wish…"

"I know it isn't easy for you not to know exactly what to do."

He smiled sheepishly. "Transparent, am I?"

"We should try to be."

He nodded solemnly. "You're right. Come on." He ushered her over to the couch and they sat, curling into each other, reminding Sierra of those early days of marriage when they'd sat together and watched a show or made out happily until he'd scoop her up and take her to bed.

"I don't have answers for my family, but we'll find them. Together. I think everything that's happened… It's certainly made me aware there are times I need to, and *can,* say no to my mother. To my father. I felt for so long I owed them this perfect son, and I'm not even sure *why* I felt that way. Maybe it was just easy because it meant *I* didn't have to make decisions. I didn't have to risk failure. I'm not sure I would have ever realized that if we hadn't talked last night."

"It was hard, and I'm sorry I ran away. You were right. I do it when it matters. When I think failing will hurt more than anything. But that's silly, because it's not like it's life or death. I need to be stronger." She reached out and touched his cheek. It was bristled with a day's worth of growth now and he looked a little rumpled.

It felt right somehow, her perfectly tidy husband all rumpled and messed up. Because love meant being uncomfortable sometimes and not doing or looking or feeling like you'd choose to.

He grabbed her hand and pulled it from his face, then grabbed her other and held them together between his, so earnest and that fierceness still. "I want you to tell me, when it hurts. When you need me. I need you to tell me, even if I don't get it. Even if you need to knock some sense into me. I need help, Sierra. Help to get it right. I never thought I did, but I can't figure it all out on my own."

"You're right. I thought love would be easy, effortless, but that isn't it at all. It's the thing you work the hardest for because it's the most worth it. But I need you to tell me when you're hurt, too. I tried to reach out at first when you'd found out about your father, but you were so cold, so shut off. Then I found out you didn't confide in me. You *lied* to me and let me find out at that awful meeting, and I just… It hurt. It wounded me. I was afraid to say something because I thought that would end it, and then it ended anyway so that was stupid. And I know… Looking *back*, I know you wouldn't have pushed me further away if I'd told you it hurt me."

"But maybe I would have," he said, shaking his head sadly. "Because I was so sure I had to figure out how I felt, file it away and know what to do before I could talk it over with you. With anyone. I didn't want you to have to... I thought it would be wrong of me to lay that at your feet."

"It might have scared me. It might have been too much. Maybe I wouldn't have handled it right. God, we have an awful lot to learn, don't we?"

"I think..." He took a deep breath and let it out. "As long as we want to learn it together, we'll get through the rough spots. The mistakes. As long as we always come back to this place right here where we talk it out. Because I love you, Sierra. I never, ever want to come that close to losing you again."

"I love you too," she whispered since her throat was so tight. Then, to really get their new start off on the right foot, she admitted the other prevalent feeling in her chest. "And I'm scared."

He pulled her into his arms, onto his lap, holding her close and tight. "I'll keep you safe," he whispered into her ear.

"We'll keep each other safe," she whispered, leaning in to him, relaxing fully for the first time in months.

Because it wouldn't be perfect or easy or happy, but it would be a good marriage full of hard work, hope, and love.

Chapter Fourteen

A month later

SIERRA KEPT PRESSING her hand to her stomach. Not in the way she usually did these days, trying to find some evidence of the baby growing somewhere in there. Tonight, she was nervous.

Not that she could pinpoint why. She loved parties, and rather enjoyed being the center of attention, which her and Carter would no doubt would be.

But Dr. McArthur and Mrs. McArthur were going to be there and Sierra wasn't sure she was prepared for whatever their reaction was going to be. She and Carter had decided to keep their distance from his parents while they worked on getting their marriage back on track. He saw his father at the hospital, and occasionally went and had lunch with his mother on his lunch break.

But it wouldn't always be that easy to simply keep their distance. They lived too close, and Carter's life was too entwined with theirs through the hospital. Besides, the McArthurs weren't evil.

Whether Sierra liked it or not, they were her unborn baby's grandparents. Which meant, loath as she was to admit it, she had to try to find some peace with them. Maybe, like a marriage relationship, that would take some giving pieces of herself she didn't necessarily want to give.

She shook her head. Some other day she'd worry about that. These days, she took worry one step at a time. And tonight wasn't about worry. It was about celebrating.

"Oh, don't you look pretty," Kaitlin exclaimed, stepping into the living room. She was wearing a pretty sundress herself, though she had a baby blanket draped over her shoulder. Ellie was settled on her hip in an adorable purple dress with ruffles and layers.

Sierra would be happy whether her baby turned out to be a boy or a girl, but having a girl to dress up, a girl who could be a friend to Ellie… Oh, that would be sweet.

"Thanks. My hair's okay?"

Kaitlin nodded and Sierra ran her hand over her white dress. She still wasn't showing, and Kaitlin was still the only one who knew, but that would change soon.

The white lace she was wearing wasn't anything as elaborate as her first wedding dress had been, and this wasn't really a *wedding* per se. It was a renewal. An announcement. A surprise for just about everyone in attendance.

"Mom's not going to approve of the extravagance."

"Mom's going to hear *second grandbaby* and not care about anything else," Kaitlin reassured.

Sierra smiled. "I'm so glad we're telling everyone. Secrets

are *not* fun."

"Let me see again."

Sierra went over to her purse on the table and pulled out the sonogram picture. It was just a viability scan, no clue as to the sex yet, but it still gave Sierra something tangible to hold on to. This little blob was in her, growing just as he or she should be.

Ellie babbled and waved her chubby fists and Sierra couldn't believe her life was going to have *this* at the end of the year. It still seemed so very far away.

"We should get out there. Everyone had arrived when I came in to change Ellie. Carter's with the officiant and said to come out whenever you're ready."

"I look okay?" Sierra wasn't usually so needy in the reassurance department when it came to her looks, but it seemed easier to worry about how she looked than how this was all going to go.

"You look gorgeous."

"Okay." She walked with her sister to the back of the house. Carter and Cole had spent most of the afternoon decorating the backyard themselves. Fairy lights and streamers. Nothing extravagant. Nothing that would tip people off that they were attending something other than an anniversary party.

When she stepped out the sliding glass door, Carter's back was to her. He was wearing a suit, though it was more a khaki color than anything dark or heavy. He was standing with Cole, Luke, and Beckett, who were dressed more casually in jeans and button-up shirts and boots, talking about something or other. She liked that the families could mingle like that, even if it was only the younger generation.

She surveyed the rest of the group. Jess and Lina were huddled together laughing about something. Her parents were together on a bench, talking to each other and laughing. They looked relaxed and happy, more so than she was used to seeing them. That was nice. A reassurance of sorts. Sometimes she hadn't figured her parents loved each other very much, but she saw it clear as day now. Maybe they'd had their own problems, but had worked through them. Just as she and Carter had.

Sierra smiled at the thought and glanced over to where Dr. and Mrs. McArthur sat on two lawn chairs, somewhat removed from the group. They weren't talking to each other. Instead they were looking around imperiously.

Sierra almost felt sorry for them, but then Carter turned around and his easy smile widened when his gaze met hers. After that, she didn't think about anything or anyone else except the man who crossed to her.

She held him off as he approached. "Don't you dare kiss me when my makeup is perfect."

He leaned forward, though didn't kiss her as she'd half feared, half hoped. Instead, he lowered his mouth to her ear. "Well, I'll save messing it up for later, then."

It sent a delightful shiver through her and then he was

grinning down at her, which just made her feel soft, and happy. She'd noted that they both smiled a lot more lately. It wasn't all joy and happiness, like she'd originally thought marriage should be, but it was a lot easier to be happy when you were talking than when you weren't. It even managed to make the normal happy a little brighter.

"Ready?" he asked, excitement clear as day on his face.

She nodded as Carter slipped his arm around her waist, his excitement almost settling most of her nerves.

"Everyone? If I could have your attention here for a few moments."

Slowly the small group of McArthurs and Shullers quieted and turned their attention to Carter.

"We want to thank you all for coming," Carter said, his arm firm around her waist. She leaned into him, always so impressed at how good he was in front of a crowd. "I know we billed this as an anniversary party, but it's a little bit more than that."

The small group of their family murmured amongst themselves, and Sierra was glad they'd done it this way. Keeping to themselves over the past month, wanting to really build their foundation. But they were ready to start spending more time outside themselves, and especially make strides with both their families to build workable, respectful relationships.

"Sierra and I didn't just want to celebrate the first year of our marriage, we wanted to recommit ourselves to it. Symbolically. In front of all of you, in our home. So, we're going to have a short renewal of vows ceremony, and while we considered doing it just the two of us, we really wanted our families to be a part of it. Most of you know because you're doing it yourselves, but marriage isn't easy, and having a supportive family is so much of what got us through the past few months."

"I would have been lost without my mom, Jess, Lina, and most especially Kaitlin," Sierra said, feeling oddly teary. She'd never expected her thank you to make her cry, but it was hard to put into words how much it meant that she'd been able to turn to all four women and find the woman she wanted to be in the midst of it. "You four supported me, gave me amazing advice, and were just there when I needed it. It means the world to me."

"And I have to do something I never thought I'd do, which is credit my younger brother's advice and my little sister's help with waking me up from a very insular, selfish space. Cole, Lina, thank you. I'd be lost without you."

The people being thanked looked on, a wide variety of expressions, though they all registered some amount of shock and quite a bit of pride.

Carter cleared his throat. "So, if you'll all find a seat." He gestured for the officiant and Sierra and Carter moved to the place they'd practiced earlier. Carter took her hands as they faced each other, and the officiant began.

"Carter, Sierra, you've decided to renew your vows on

this beautiful evening, not making new promises to each other, but repeating old ones with better knowledge of what they mean. In front of your families, friends, and God, do you recommit to each other, promise to love, cherish, communicate, for as long as you both shall live?"

"I do," Carter said, smiling and squeezing her hands.

"I do, too," Sierra echoed, giving his hands a squeeze back. It was simple, but it was all she'd wanted. A little symbol for them to carry around in their hearts, and love surrounding them while they did it.

They turned back to the crowd who gave an enthusiastic round of applause with a few cheers and whistles.

Carter cleared his throat. "There's just one more thing."

Everyone paused in their moves to congratulate the happy couple.

"Since we're celebrating love and futures, we want to announce..." Carter turned his gaze to her so she brought her hand to her stomach.

"We will be a family of three come November."

"I knew it," Mom yelled, delighted and making everyone else laugh. Then it was a throng, everyone coming up with hugs and congratulations. Mom cried all over her and even Dad seemed emotional. Jess and Lina chatted excitedly and hugged her a few million times.

When Dr. McArthur and Mrs. McArthur came up to them, Sierra braced herself for... Well, something unpleasant.

"Congratulations, Carter," Dr. McArthur said holding out his hand.

Carter shook it. "Thank you. And congratulations to you too, Grandpa."

Dr. McArthur looked almost taken aback for a second. He quickly recovered himself, but Sierra felt something close to warmth from the cold man for the first time. Maybe it was a sign of things to come.

She glanced at Mrs. McArthur, waiting for something a little more scathing. But Mrs. McArthur tried to smile. At least, that's what Sierra *thought* the older woman's mouth was doing.

"Congratulations. I'm very pleased. My first grandchild. How exciting."

Sierra didn't think Mrs. McArthur seemed *excited*, but she was trying to be civil, which was a first. Maybe it was the hormones, maybe it was just the sheer joy of the whole night and being able to come through all that ugliness to be here in this moment of perfect happiness, but she reached out and gave Mrs. McArthur a quick hug.

When she released Mrs. McArthur, the couple quickly moved off and toward the table of refreshments. Sierra turned to Carter.

"Did that just happen? You hugged my mother."

"She seemed to need it."

He shook his head, then lowered his mouth to hers. "Fair warning. I'm about to ruin your makeup."

"Hm. I guess I'll allow it." And she let the man she loved kiss her in front of their friends and family, with their child growing in her stomach. If perfect days existed, she'd found hers, and she'd remember it forever.

November 2016

"It's going to be all right."

Sierra shook her head. "It isn't. Because it isn't possible. It's not going to come out. It's not."

"She'll be out soon enough," Carter soothed. "Just breathe." Outside he was calm, cool. A doctor who knew how these things went.

Underneath his shirt he was sweating and a little afraid Sierra was right, even though as a doctor he knew it wasn't physically possible. Their baby *would* come out. He held Sierra's hand as she pushed through another contraction. His heart couldn't seem to beat normally and he felt a little lightheaded.

He'd never expected the whole experience to be overwhelming considering he had at least some experience on the medical side of things. But it was something else to watch your wife struggle. To hurt. Mixed in with the smells and the sounds and he didn't know how she hadn't passed out.

How he hadn't.

"She isn't coming out. This won't work. I can't do it,"

Sierra moaned in a rush of breath after another long push. She looked absolutely miserable in the hospital bed, her hair pulled back, her face red and sweaty. She'd had an epidural but it hadn't seemed to take away the pain like it was supposed to, and now it was too late to fix that.

"You *can* do it," Carter assured her. He squeezed her hand and wiped the sweat off her face and prayed like hell that she would actually do it because this was agony.

If he admitted to her that *he* felt agony, he was pretty sure she'd manage to physically harm him even in the midst of labor.

She shook her head, but with the next contraction she took a deep breath and pushed and moaned. Carter felt helpless next to her, but he held on to her and said any encouraging word he could think of.

"We're almost there," the doctor assured Sierra. "Just another push or two."

"I can't. I can't."

"Come on, baby. One more good push and then we'll get to meet her and decide on that name."

Sierra let out a breath that sounded more like a sob, which nearly cut Carter in half. They were never doing this again. It was too awful.

"That's it, that's it," the doctor urged. In a moment that was something like a blur, there was suddenly the odd little wail of a baby. The doctor pulled out the wriggling mass and immediately put her to Sierra's stomach.

They both looked down at the wrinkly little thing, still messy. He'd seen this, done this as the doctor putting the baby on the mother, but that didn't prepare him for seeing *his* daughter.

"Look at her," Sierra whispered, stroking a hand down her cheek. "She's real."

"And tiny."

"And perfect." Sierra looked up at him, tears in her eyes. "I know we had two names picked out, but I came up with a third last night."

"What's that?" Carter asked idly, looking down at *his daughter* on his wife's chest. His. Theirs.

"We'll get her all cleaned up now, okay?" the nurse said, picking up the baby and wiping up the mess.

"Okay," Sierra agreed reluctantly, watching with desperate eyes as they moved to the other side of the room and cleaned the baby up and measured and weighed her.

"Six pounds, ten ounces," the nurse announced cheerfully. "Twenty inches long. She's looking good, Mom and Dad."

"Six pounds, ten ounces," Sierra repeated.

"Mom and Dad," Carter repeated.

They looked at each other then and half laughed, half sobbed.

Carter pressed a kiss to her forehead. "You were amazing. Perfect. Strong and—"

"I wanted to give up."

"The great thing about childbirth is it's really hard to give up halfway through."

She sank back into her pillows, clearly exhausted even as her eyes watched the nurses.

"What was the name you came up with?" he asked, still standing next to her bed and holding her hand. He wanted to collapse into a heap, but he couldn't seem to take his hand away from Sierra.

"Kaylin. Some of Kaitlin's name, some of Lina's. Then maybe we can work Jess's name into the middle name. Jessmin. Jess and Mindy, like my mom. Would that make your mom mad to not have her name in there?"

"We don't have to tell her."

Sierra smiled a little at that. "What do you think? Kaylin Jessmin McArthur. Even Dr. Kaylin McArthur sounds good."

Carter laughed. "Oh, so you're going to be the doctor pusher, huh?"

"She can be whatever she wants," Sierra said, holding her arms out as the nurse handed Kaylin over, bundled in a blanket with a little pink knitted hat on her head. It even had a bow on the front. "But I bet she'll want to be like her daddy."

Daddy. He was a *daddy* now, and this amazing little being was *his*. To love, to protect, to raise. Maybe his earlier proclamation of never doing this again was a little premature, he decided as dark blue eyes looked out at him from under a knit cap. Maybe they could do this a few more times.

Because he'd learned how to be a husband, with the help of his family and his wife, so he had no doubt he could learn how to be a pretty fine dad.

With Sierra at his side, there wasn't a doubt in his mind.

Epilogue

Present-day Marietta

SIERRA SAT IN the uncomfortable plastic chair of the hospital waiting room, about at her wit's end trying to keep Kaylin occupied without touching every germy surface in the place.

"We should have waited," Sierra said to Carter as Kaylin fussed and tried to wriggle out of her lap.

Carter pawed through the baby bag trying to find a toy that would hold Kaylin's interest. "Cole said it'd be any minute now. You said you wanted to be here."

"I should have realized waiting with a one-and-a-half-year-old would be like waiting with a rabid octopus."

Carter grinned at her. "Rabid octopus. Now, that's a new one."

"Pam-paw!" As Dr. McArthur and Mrs. McArthur approached, Sierra let Kaylin down. The one-and-a-half-year-old toddled over to Dr. McArthur and wrapped her pudgy arms around his legs.

His MS had progressed a little aggressively in the past few months, so he didn't pick her up, but he did give her head a pat and greet her cheerfully. Mrs. McArthur reached down and took Kaylin's hand.

Kaylin babbled happily up at her grandparents, and Sierra didn't catch any of the words she seemed to be picking up at a rapid pace, but Kaylin was more than happy to hold court.

It was still strange, even all this time later, to watch the McArthurs interact with her child. Sierra's relationship with them wasn't roses and rainbows. It was polite, at best, but the McArthurs had proved to be good grandparents. They'd only overstepped a few times, and Carter always told them to back off, and they did. It had taken trial and error, a few arguments, and things weren't perfect, but they were good. Sierra hadn't really sat back and fully realized that until right now watching them entertain Kaylin while they waited.

"Did I miss it?" Lina was breathless and red-cheeked as she jogged into the waiting room.

"We haven't heard anything yet," Sierra assured her. "Where's Ace?" Jess's brother, who was also Lina's soon-to-be husband, was supposed to have been coming with Lina from where they lived outside of Kalispell.

"He's parking the car. Of course we wasted five minutes arguing who should. It's really not fair my niece or nephew is also my fiancé's niece or nephew. I have no seniority or pull," Lina grumbled.

Kaylin made an indescribable noise they'd all decided was her attempt at saying Lina. Lina scooped her up, making the toddler squeal. "Stop growing, shortcake. You're making me sad I don't get to visit more often."

The door that led into the labor and delivery rooms opened and Cole stepped out, broad grin taking up the entire width of his face.

"It's a boy," Cole announced, looking awed and exhausted all at once. He and Jess had decided not to find out the sex of the baby beforehand, or at least not tell anyone, so it was a surprise for everyone waiting.

"Now, isn't that good news. Some testosterone for the next generation," Dr. McArthur offered.

"And what's this boy's name?" Sierra asked, feeling a little choked up over how excited Cole looked. Bringing a new life into the world was such an awing experience even when it wasn't yours.

She remembered how transformative it had been to watch Carter learn how to be a father, especially in those first few days. What a magical, exhausting time it was.

"Colton Finn McArthur." He winked at Carter. "Another C-name for the McArthur books."

"Can we see?" Lina asked impatiently.

Cole nodded. "Not everyone all at once though. The room isn't that big and Jess wants to see everyone, but she's exhausted too. Mom and Dad, Lina and—"

Ace jogged through the waiting room doors, as out of breath as Lina had been. "Well?"

"We've got a nephew," Lina announced excitedly. "Can

we go first?" she said, turning to Cole hopefully as she handed Kaylin off to Sierra.

"Jess asked for you both. You can come in with Mom and Dad, if Sierra and Carter can wait?"

"No problem," Carter offered. "Congratulations, Daddy."

"Hell," Cole muttered. "Why does that one word about knock a person over?"

"It's something else."

The four of them filed back after Cole, leaving her and Carter and Kaylin in the waiting room alone for the moment.

Carter leaned his head against hers. "We could have another, you know."

Sierra turned to look at her husband, trying not to grin. She kept her expression bland, her gaze cool. "Could we?"

"You probably want to make sure the summer camp goes off without a hitch first."

She had to smile at that. She'd become friends with an art teacher at the high school and together they'd started putting together a community summer art program. It had taken almost two years to launch, and this summer would be their inaugural year.

Carter had been ridiculously supportive, and her mother had been babysitter extraordinaire these past six months, allowing Sierra some of the time and freedom to help get everything put together.

"That'd be good. I think it's... Well, it's going to go well one way or another, but I want to feel present while we're doing it. I don't want to be puking my guts out."

"Oh, weren't those the days?"

She chuckled. "But in the fall, Kaylin creeping up on two. That'd put them about the same amount of years between you and Cole."

"Does that bode well?" Carter asked, only half joking. "I don't recall me being that close to my siblings growing up."

"But look at us now." Sierra gave him a quick peck on the cheek. "We're pretty good at getting along these days. We'll set a good example. Besides, this one needs something to keep her occupied. Torturing a younger sibling might just be it."

Kaylin was busy pulling every single thing out of her baby bag and throwing it across the floor.

They exchanged a look that communicated both love and exasperation over their strong-willed daughter. It made Sierra smile because it reminded her of a time when she'd thought she and Carter just weren't wired the same way as married couples who could share a look.

But it turned out, shared looks and nonverbal communication took work, and time, things they'd both put into their marriage a lot over the past couple years.

And it was a good one. They both got down on their hands and knees and began to clean up Kaylin's mess, much to her dismay. Working together they got all their belongings back in the bag and talked Kaylin down from her tantrum.

Carter was holding her on his shoulders to distract her from the trashcan she wanted to play with when Ace, Lina, Dr. McArthur and Mrs. McArthur came back out.

"They said to send you three right back," Lina said, sounding cheerful even though she looked teary. She and Ace were holding hands, and so were Dr. McArthur and Mrs. McArthur.

It was funny to think how they were all McArthurs, all of them, somehow a family at this point. They'd never be precisely the image so many people had of them, but in the course of a few years they'd all learned how to be better versions of themselves.

So, Sierra walked back to the hospital room to meet her new nephew, and introduce Kaylin to her new cousin, with all the hope in the world for the future generations of McArthurs and all the love they would have and, most importantly, share.

The End

To Read about the Couples Who Appear in *Bride for Keeps*...

Kaitlin & Beckett: Bride by Mistake
Cole & Jess: Keep Me, Cowboy
Lina & Ace: Ignite

The Big Sky Brides Series

Book 1: *Bride by Mistake*

Book 2: *Bride for Keeps*

Available now at your favorite online retailer!

More by Nicole Helm

Keep Me, Cowboy
Cole McArthur's story

Ignite
Lina McArthur's story

Available now at your favorite online retailer!

About the Author

Nicole Helm writes down-to-earth contemporary romance—from farmers to cowboys, midwest to *the* west, she writes stories about people finding themselves and finding love in the process. She lives in Missouri with her husband and two sons, surrounded by light sabers, video games, and a shared dream of someday owning a farm.

Visit her website at NicoleHelm.wordpress.com

Thank you for reading

Bride for Keeps

If you enjoyed this book, you can find more from all our great authors at TulePublishing.com, or from your favorite online retailer.

TULE
PUBLISHING